W9-AHM-689

# FERN MICHAELS

# NO PLACE LIKE HOME

POCKET BOOKS
New York  London  Toronto  Sydney

Pocket Books
A Division of Simon & Schuster, Inc.
1230 Avenue of the Americas
New York, NY 10020

This book is a work of fiction. Names, characters, places, and incidents either are products of the author's imagination or are used fictitiously. Any resemblance to actual events or locales or persons, living or dead, is entirely coincidental.

This Pocket Books paperback edition November 2010

POCKET and colophon are registered trademarks of Simon & Schuster, Inc.

For information about special discounts for bulk purchases, please contact Simon & Schuster Special Sales at 1-866-506-1949 or business@simonandschuster.com

The Simon & Schuster Speakers Bureau can bring authors to your live event. For more information or to book an event contact the Simon & Schuster Speakers Bureau at 1-866-248-3049 or visit our website at www.simonspeakers.com

Cover art by Robert Grantt Steele

Manufactured in the United States of America

10  9  8  7  6  5  4  3  2  1

ISBN 978-1-4516-0939-4
ISBN 978-0-7434-7718-5 (ebook)

# Prologue

~ · ~ · ~

Loretta Cisco, founder and CEO of Cisco Candies, opened the screen door leading to the back porch, Freddie, her golden retriever, at her side. The door squeaked and groaned just the way an old screen door is supposed to creak and groan. Just the way her old bones creaked and groaned, she thought. A smile tugged at the corners of her mouth.

It was autumn, her favorite time of the year. Even though she couldn't see the gold-and-bronze leaves because of the milky white cataracts covering her eyes, she could *smell* the air in the foothills of the Allegheny Mountains. To her, autumn had its own distinctive smell, just as the other seasons did.

She knew where every tree, every bush, every flower, every twig was. After all, she'd lived her entire life here in the rich foothills of the mountains. Oh, she had a fancy apartment in New York, where Cisco Candies had its corporate offices, and yes, she visited it twice a year. But it had never been *home.* Home was this winterized cottage she'd expanded and improved upon. She even had a big, old barn where she kept her car, her grandchildren's three red jet skis on their trailer, their mountain bikes, snowmobiles, sleds, winter skis, water skis, Sam's canoe and all his mountain-climbing equipment, and all the gear a set of triplets needed to get through their young lives. She knew where everything was in the barn, too, because when she got lonely, she'd walk out there with Freddie, touch the various things, and her memories would surface. More often than not, she cried.

Loretta walked across the porch, past the four Adirondack chairs with the heavy padding, past the round table with the hurricane lamp in the middle, until she was at the top of the steps. Freddie inched her closer to the railing. She smiled as she carefully descended the four steps to the garden path. Her hands reached out to touch the holly bushes. She had four. Most people didn't know you needed a male and a female bush to get the lush red berries that were so precious at Christmastime. Her hands worked at the prickly leaves until she felt the different sprays of berries. The berries were probably still green and would not turn red till around November. They felt full and lush this year. She wished she could see them, for she loved holly, especially the variegated kind. For sure they would have fresh holly in the house for the holidays.

She bent down at the end of the holly row to let her fingers touch the velvety petals of the chrysanthemums, which were as big and round as bushel baskets. She hoped they looked vibrant this year. There were four that were a deep purple in color, two lemon yellow, and nine bronze with gold tips. They were almost as old as she was. She wondered how many people knew you had to pinch the suckers off the plants to make them grow round and fat. Just like you had to pinch them off tomato plants. She hadn't known it either until a neighbor told her.

She continued her walk to the little garden she'd planted when the triplets were born. Freddie nudged her leg again, signaling her that she was slightly off course. Three birch trees. Her son had carved all their initials in the spindly trunks, which had expanded over the years. Her hands could no longer encompass them and the initials were still there. Jonathan had said he wanted their names to withstand time and the elements, Sara, Hannah, and Sam. Then hers, and Jonathan's, and, of course, Margie's. She'd always felt a little guilty over those three trees, wondering why she'd never planted one when her son was born. The best answer she could come up with was, it had been a different time, and people had thought differently back then. Her touch was reverent as her fingers traced the carvings. So many years ago.

"Let's check out the pumpkin patch, Freddie. The temperature is starting to drop, and I can feel the sun starting to fade." She walked slowly, savoring the warmth of the late-afternoon sun. "Ah, we're here. Show me where they are, Freddie. Oh, I wish I could see them. I guess I have to get down on my knees and feel around." She'd planted six pumpkin plants in the early spring, the way she did every year. Her eyes hadn't been so bad back then. On her knees, her arms stretched out, she counted them. Nineteen pumpkins, each as big as a beach ball. When the triplets were little, they'd carved them all and lined them up along the driveway, the candles in the center glowing brightly in the dark night. The triplets were in college now and didn't come home for Halloween. She still planted the pumpkins, though; she thought of it as a tradition rather than a habit.

It was Sam who loved to toast the seeds. Sometimes he put sugar on them, sometimes salt. Then, when he was all finished, Sara and Hannah would snatch them away. Sam was so good-natured, he'd just shake his head and make another batch.

Loretta dusted off her hands and knees. The wind picked up, ruffling her snow-white hair. She looked up, knowing she was standing under the old sycamore where they picnicked every year. Her voice cracked slightly when her hand reached down to pat her loyal companion. "I love this place, Freddie. I think I would die if I ever had to leave here. My whole life is here, along with all my memories. I wouldn't know what to do someplace else." Freddie barked to show she understood as she guided her mistress back up the garden path to the back porch.

When she reached the top of the steps and walked past the four Adirondack chairs, she stopped to smell the air. Someone over the hill, probably the new neighbor she'd heard about, was burning leaves. She dearly loved the smell. Another memory.

Her kitchen wasn't modern like the ones she saw in the glossy magazines because she didn't want a shiny state-of-the-art kitchen. It wasn't that she didn't like new things, she did, but this kitchen was hers and she simply liked it the way it was. She'd laughed there, cried there, comforted her son and grandchildren there. It was where they'd congregated after her daughter-in-law's funeral. It was where they sat holding hands, wondering how they were going to go on without Margie. They did go on because they had no other choice.

Loretta poured herself a cup of coffee and carried it to the old scarred table that could sit eight comfortably.

It was a large, old-fashioned kitchen. Maybe that's why she loved it so. The stove was old, with six burners and pilot lights that miraculously never went out. The oven was just warm enough to dry the orange peels and cinnamon sticks she replenished from time to time. The scent carried through the old house, even to the second floor. The triplets said they loved coming into the house because they loved the smell. The refrigerator was an old-timer, too, big enough to hold enough food for an army. The triplets, her son, Freddie, and herself were her army. The heavy-duty dishwasher was her only concession to what she called modern wizardry. She only used it when the triplets were home. The cabinets were painted white, with beveled glass insets. The windows, and there were six of them, were diamond-paned and adorned with red-and-white-checkered curtains. They probably needed to be washed by now because she hadn't touched them since she did her spring cleaning. The floor was old, craggy, and ridged, heart of pine. It was beautiful because she'd cared for it lovingly. She knew every crack, every ridge, every knothole. Rag rugs she'd braided herself were by the sink and stove. When it was time to clean them, she hung them over the banister on the back porch, hosed them off with soapy water, and let them dry in the sun. They were old, too, at least thirty years or more.

She walked around the big, old kitchen, touching the bright ceramic apple that held Freddie's chews instead of cookies. The triplets had made the apple at summer camp one year. Her hands reached out to touch the raised hearth that was arm level with her rocker. In the winter she planted seedlings and kept the little clay pots in the corner where it was nice and warm and got just the right amount of sun from the nearby window.

There probably wouldn't be any seedlings this year. There probably wouldn't be a garden either.

What she loved most about her kitchen was the cavernous fireplace that took up one whole wall of the room. In the winter months, she spent most of her time right there in the kitchen, rocking in her mother's old rocker, knitting scarves no one ever wore. When her vision had turned bad, she'd stopped knitting and started to listen to books on tape. She had tons of them, thanks to the triplets. One of Freddie's five beds was next to Loretta's rocker, along with a pile of her toys. Sometimes they both slept in the kitchen—she in her rocker, Freddie in her bed.

Loretta finished her coffee. It was time to start dinner. First she removed the tray with the orange peels and cinnamon sticks from the oven. She leaned over to listen to the click of the oven switch. It was one click for 325 degrees and two clicks for 350. When she heard the second click, she lowered the oven door and turned to the refrigerator. She withdrew two trays. Meat loaf, mashed potatoes, peas and carrots, and cauliflower. She added two biscuits from a Ziploc bag and placed the trays in the oven.

It was time to wash up for dinner, and time to *listen* to the six o'clock news on the television.

It was after eight o'clock when Loretta put

away the last dish, let Freddie out, and then changed into her nightgown and robe, and let Freddie back in. She was going to sit on the rocker and listen to a new book on tape her grandson Sam had sent her.

Another day was coming to a close.

Before Loretta settled herself in the rocker, she reached into the cookie jar for one of Freddie's rawhide chews. Now they were ready to settle down for the night. No, not quite. She needed the portable phone her son had given her last year. He'd programmed it, too. She didn't have to dial a number, just press 1, 2, or 3. The number 1 on the dial was Jonathan himself, the triplets were number 2, and Harry Nathan, her doctor, was number 3. It was unlikely anyone would call her. Jonathan was too busy, or so he said, and the triplets called every day at noon, so they wouldn't be calling again at night. Harry Nathan never called. Secretly she suspected he couldn't remember she was his patient. She really needed to think about getting a new doctor, a young, savvy one who didn't creak and moan and groan. All the rest of her friends were either gone or living in retirement villages, hoping relatives would visit or call. At least once in a while.

If she kept this up, she was going to start feeling sorry for herself, then she would end up crying herself to sleep.

Maybe if she'd listened to her own advice, she wouldn't have cried and wouldn't have slipped on the braided rug by the sink when she went to get the portable phone. One second she was standing upright, the phone in her hand, the next she was on the floor, her arm pinned under her chest. Pain ricocheted up her arm.

She knew her arm was probably broken. In the time it took her heart to beat twice, she knew her life was never going to be the same. Freddie licked Loretta's face and whimpered at her side. *God in heaven, what will happen to my beloved dog?* She did her best to slide backward so that her back rested against the cabinet under the sink.

With her good hand she placed the portable phone in her lap, her finger tracing the numbers. She pressed the number 3 and waited until she heard Harry Nathan's reedy voice. "It's Loretta, Harry. I think I broke my arm. I'm going to need some medical attention. Of course I want you to come out here. I'm blind with cataracts, Harry, or did you forget? Do you expect me to get in a car and drive to you? Of course I'll wait for you. Where could I possibly go?"

Loretta drew a deep breath before she pressed the number 1. She really didn't think her son would be home, and he wasn't. She left a message. She wouldn't call the triplets because they'd drop everything, pile into their car, and drive there at ninety miles an hour. They would do it because they loved her. She wondered, as she struggled with the pain, how long it would take her son to arrive. *If* he arrived.

Freddie barked thirty minutes later at the sound of a car pulling up to the house, but she didn't leave her mistress's side.

Harry Nathan was a small, stooped man, with a short beard and wire-rimmed glasses. He looked down at his patient. "This is a fine mess, Loretta. How many times this past year did I tell you to get yourself a live-in housekeeper? Well?"

Long years of familiarity allowed Loretta to snap at her doctor. "Shut up, Harry, and help me. I guess we have to go to the clinic, is that it?"

"No, we are not going to my clinic. I'm too old to be setting bones. I'm taking you to the hospital."

"Fine, but I'm not staying there, so get that idea right out of your head. You wait for me and bring me back here. Do we understand each other, Harry? The reason I have to come back tonight is Freddie. Swear to me, Harry."

"All right, all right. Here, let me help you up. Now, where are your insurance cards?"

"In my purse. Put my afghan over my shoulders. I can't put my coat on."

Three hours later Freddie whooped her

pleasure when Dr. Harry Nathan ushered his patient back into the house. "She's rocky, Freddie, so I think we'll let her sleep it off on this rocker," he said, helping Loretta get comfortable.

"Loretta, I'm going to leave two pills on a saucer, and a glass of water on the hearth. You won't have to get up that way. You're going to have some pain, so be prepared. I want you to call me if things get bad. I'll check on you in the morning. I'm thinking we can take those cataracts off in a few months."

"Go home, Harry, and let me sleep. Is Freddie all right?"

When Freddie took her place next to Loretta, Harry turned off the lights, leaving only a night-light on in the kitchen and the light in the hall leading to the downstairs bathroom. He patted Loretta's shoulder, and said softly, "It's hell getting old, my friend, but it beats the alternative. Sleep well." He let himself out quietly. Tomorrow was *not* going to be a good day, he could feel it in his bones.

\* \* \*

Jonathan Cisco arrived at noon the following day. His jaw was grim, his eyes furious as he stalked his way into the kitchen, where his mother was sitting in the rocker. He wasted no time. "I told you this was going to happen, didn't I, Mom? Why didn't you listen to me? Dr. Nathan and I both urged you to get a live-in but you wouldn't hear of it. This is what happens when you don't listen. Now, until those cataracts come off, you're going to Laurel Hills where you can be looked after properly. I don't want any more calls in the middle of the night. I have a lot on my plate right now, Mom, and I don't want to have to worry about you hurting yourself."

Loretta reared up in her chair. "It wasn't the middle of the night. It wasn't even nine o'clock, and I am not going to that stainless steel assisted-living facility. Get that idea right out of your head. This is my house, and I'm not leaving. Go away, Jonathan. I'm sorry I called you. You have no idea how sorry I am."

"You're going, Mom, even if I have to carry you. I arranged everything. It wasn't easy either. You can take Freddie with you. That took some doing, but I managed. I'm going to pack your things, and that's my last word. Tell me what you want to take with you."

"Jonathan, please, I don't want to go there. I saw that place once, and it's awful. Freddie will hate it. I don't belong in a place like that. Please, son, listen to me."

"Mom, you're going, and that's final. It's for your own good."

Loretta Cisco shriveled into herself. She was beaten, and she knew it. She was blind, she had a broken arm, and she had a dog who needed to be cared for. What chance did she have against her son? None.

*I'll die there*, she thought. *I'll never see this place again*.

An hour later, she was in her son's car. They were almost to the top of the little rise above the cottage. She rolled down the window and stuck her head out. The scent of burning leaves wafted through the window. She couldn't see her beloved little cottage in the valley, but she could *smell* it. Loretta waved good-bye. Freddie threw back her head and howled. And then she barked her own good-bye.

*If this is all God is going to give me, so be it.*

# 1

≈ · ≈ · ≈

*T*he Cisco triplets stared at one another across the table, shivering inside their warm ski jackets. They ordered hot chocolate from a weary-looking waitress.

Sam, the youngest of the triplets by seven whole minutes, finally spoke. "Will somebody please tell me what the hell we're doing here in New York City, anyway? We should have gone to the mountains like we planned. I hate it that we switched up, and Cisco is spending Thanksgiving by herself. I thought we had more guts than to kowtow to our father and his new . . . squeeze."

Hard-Hearted Hannah, as she came to be known during their childhoods, punched her brother's upper arm. "We're here because Granny Cisco insisted we do what Dad said. It's one of Dad's command performances, so let's just make the best of it. It's a lousy day and a half out of our lives, okay? I think we're tough enough to handle whatever he throws at us."

Sara, a.k.a. Sassy Sara, folded her arms across her chest, still unwilling to remove her down jacket. She looked around, knowing they were causing a small stir in the coffee shop. It was uncanny the way the three of them mirrored one another. They had the same curly reddish-brown hair, the same smattering of freckles across the bridges of their noses. Their eyes were a startling blue that turned a pearl gray when something distressed them. At present their eyes were pearl gray, their well-defined jaws grim. And their noses twitched, another sign of anxiety. People did tend to stare at identical twins, and their brother looked so much like the girls that it was sometimes difficult to tell them apart when they were dressed in bulky clothing with their woolen hats on. When the caps were removed, of course, Sam stood out like a beacon, because of his close-cropped hair. Once, in their senior year in high school, Sam had let his hair grow when they did a skit pretending to be the McGuire Sisters. Not that any of their peers knew who the McGuire Sisters were, but they did bring down the house. "We're outta there the minute they serve dessert. Do either one of you have a problem with that?" Sara's tone clearly said they'd better not have a problem with it. She was the oldest by seven minutes, and as such was the ringleader of the trio.

As one, they cupped their hands around the steaming mugs of hot chocolate. As a rule, they moved in sync, and this time it was no different. They even sipped the hot drink on cue.

"I'm pissed. Not just a little bit pissed but big-time pissed," Hannah growled, menace ringing in her voice. "How could he do such an ugly thing and not tell us until after the fact? We aren't little kids anymore. We're seniors in college. We're grown-ups," she clarified, her freckles bunching into a knot over the bridge of her nose.

Sam poked at the tiny marshmallows in his cup with his index finger. His lips compressed into a tight line across his face at his sister's words. "Slapping Granny Cisco into an assisted-living facility is not my idea of a united family. We need to spring her. Why'd he do it? All I need is one reason. Just one lousy reason."

It was Sara's turn to make a comment. "Because he wants to take control of Cisco Candies without interference from Cisco. He has a new playmate now, and he probably needs to feel important. Men his age do stupid things like this when they go through a midlife crisis. I read that in a book somewhere. She's only *twenty-nine,* seven years older than we are. Cisco said Dad met her in a health club."

"The best part of this, if there is a best part, is Cisco is allowed to have Freddie with her," Hannah said, referring to her grandmother's seven-year-old golden retriever. "What I don't understand is why she couldn't continue to stay at the cottage. Hell, she could afford to have a whole team of medical people help her twenty-four/seven. So she stumbles around a little because of her cataracts, so what? I know, I know, they have to be ripe before they can be removed. She knows that cottage by heart. So she broke her arm, so what? She slipped on the kitchen rug. She's only seventy-four and not ready to be put out to pasture, which is what I think Dad wants. Why didn't she fight? Cisco has weathered all kinds of storms, but she caved on this. I just don't get it." She was so breathless in her anger, she deflated like a pricked balloon.

"Damn it, Hanny, she didn't fight because Dad blindsided her. She didn't see it coming. No pun intended. Her own son, our father, did that to her, and he broke her heart by doing it. His explanation was, it was for her own good. He said broken bones at her age never mend properly, and he didn't want to feel responsible if she took another tumble.

"Dad also said the cottage is so isolated Cisco could take a bad fall and no one would know because she's too stubborn to have help. We all know she refuses to wear her hearing aids. He made a big deal out of that, too. He got three doctors to sign off on it and was prepared to go to court if Cisco balked. She just caved, it's that simple. You do that when someone breaks your heart. I say we take off the next semester and stay with her at the cottage. Let's take a vote."

"Yesss," Hannah and Sam said, their fists shooting in the air.

"Okay. Now, which one of us is going to break the news to good old Dad?"

"You're the oldest. Take a guess," Hannah said.

"Okay. Before or after dinner?"

"Let's play it by ear. We'll know when the time is right. I want to make sure we're straight on something. We're going home for Christmas, right? Who cares what Dad and his nubile squeeze do. We spring Cisco and take her back home even if we have to kid-nap her, right?" Sam's face was so fierce, his siblings reached out to him as they nodded.

"That's right, little brother. We've never missed a Christmas with Cisco yet, and this is not the year to start," Sara said tightly. Three hands slapped down on the table, one covering the other. "If Dad has other plans, we can live with it."

"It's time to go," Hannah said, fishing money out of her pocket to pay for the hot chocolate. "I can't wait to see what this one looks like," she said, referring to her father's latest companion. "Anyone want to bet she has big tits, collagen lips, and a tight ass?"

"That's a sucker bet," Sam snarled as he struggled with his backpack, gloves, and jacket.

Hannah shrugged into her jacket, aware that the other customers were staring at them. Their smiles were forced as they left the warm, steamy coffee shop for the walk to their grandmother's apartment at the Dakota, the historic apartment building on Manhattan's Upper West Side.

Forty-five minutes later, they rode the elevator to the ninth floor. Hannah reached into her pocket for her key.

"Forget it, the locks have probably been changed," Sara said. "We ring the bell and wait. Don't you get it, we're guests now? It's a whole new ball game this time around."

"I don't doubt you for a minute, big sister, but let's be sure. Ah, right as usual," Hannah said, withdrawing the key from the lock. She gave an elaborate shrug as she kicked the door instead of ringing the bell. When there was no response, she kicked it again, this time louder. "Look, I made a smudge," she said, pointing to an ugly black mark at the base of the door.

The door swung wide. Jonathan Cisco stared at his children. "The doorbell really does work," he said coolly. He was a tall man. A handsome man with the same curly red-brown hair as his children, and the same blue eyes. Eyes that were now pearl gray just like the triplets'. Not yet fifty, he carried his years well, in part because of his daily workouts, good eating habits, and eight hours of sleep a night, not to mention drinking the requisite eight glasses of water a day. He stood aside for the triplets to enter their grandmother's apartment. His apartment now.

"Oh myyy God!" Hannah wailed.

"I hate it!" Sara cried.

"You sure move fast, Dad," Sam said, looking around at the glaring black-and-white decor. "I never saw a black flower before. I guess you did all this redecorating before you slapped Cisco in *that place*. Looks like a major undertaking to me. Like you *planned* it way ahead of time. My opinion, for whatever it's worth, is it's ugly."

Hannah ran into the apartment and down the hall. Sara and Sam ran after her when they heard her high-pitched squeal of distress. Their eyes were wild with horror as they surveyed the three bedrooms that had at one time been theirs. Hannah's room was black and white with purple accents. Sara's was black and white with red accents. Sam's was black and white with blue accents.

"Where's our stuff?" they asked in unison. "Where's Mom's picture? The family picture with all of us in it?"

Jonathan Cisco had the grace to look ashamed. He turned away. "In storage. It was mostly just clutter. I thought since you will be graduating in the spring, you'd all be finding your own places to live. I know young college grads don't want to live with their parents."

"Now, you see, Dad, that's where you're wrong," Hard-Hearted Hannah said, living up to her childhood name. "We did plan on coming back here for as long as it takes to find really, really high-paying jobs. New York is where the job market is. What's better than paying no rent? Nothing, that's what. I want my stuff back." Her voice dripped ice. "And I damn well want Mom's picture back."

They closed ranks then and drew together. Their father realized that he would get nowhere with them. The proverbial brick wall. He shrugged as he prepared to walk out of the room.

"We want to talk about Cisco and what you did to her. She's our grandmother, and she damn well raised us, no thanks to you, Dad. How could you do that to her? How?" Sam demanded, his voice all choked up.

"I did it because it was the right thing to do. I'm sad to say your grandmother is becoming feeble. She needs to be looked after properly. She needs to eat properly, rest properly, and take her medication on time, not when and if she thinks about it. If she were to fall, she could very well become incapacitated. She couldn't handle that. She would never be the same again. I don't think any of us want that for her. I know I don't. She can't see, and she can't handle the business anymore. I'm doing her the biggest favor of her life by making sure she's safe and sound. She'll get used to the new routine at the facility. And they made a special concession for her to keep Freddie with her."

"Favor!" the triplets shouted in unison.

"This is not negotiable, and I do not have to explain to any of you why and what I do. Now, it might be a good idea for you to settle in. I have to go out now for an important meeting. I won't be home till quite late, so don't wait up for me. I hired a housekeeper some time ago, and she'll prepare dinner for you. It's nice to see you all," he added as an afterthought.

When the door closed behind their father, the triplets huddled together the way they had when they were children. Their eyes were misty with unshed tears, their bodies trembling. Hannah was the first one to speak. "I can't sleep in a black-and-white room. I need my junk. I need to see Mom's picture before I fall asleep. And I hate the color purple. Do you think he had the balls to change Cisco's room?"

They created their own wind tunnel as they raced down the hall and around the corner to their grandmother's room. Her hand shaking, Sara turned the knob. They literally wilted in relief when they saw the room was intact. "We sleep in here. Hanny and I get the bed. Sam, you get the couch. It's just as comfortable as the bed. Look, there's Freddie's bed. God, this feels so good." She bounced on the bed to make her point.

"It smells just like Cisco," Sam said inhaling deeply. "Just like her," he said happily.

Hannah swooned as she flopped down on Freddie's bed.

Sara reared up. She fiddled with her tight curly hair until she had it in a tidy bun at the nape of her neck. "We need a plan."

To Jonathan Cisco's chagrin, on Thanksgiving Day his children trooped into the dining room attired in jeans and sweatshirts that said Penn State on the front. They waited expectantly for their father to introduce the young woman at his side. "Alexandra, I'd like you to meet my children—Hannah,

Sara, and Sam." The triplets nodded, their heads barely moving.

"I've heard so much about you," Alexandra gushed. "What interesting lives you've led, and you're not yet, what is it, twenty-two?"

The triplets offered up grimaces.

"And you would be . . . how old?" Hard-Hearted Hannah asked.

"Forever twenty-nine," Alexandra said with a tight smile that didn't reach her eyes.

"What is it you do?" Sara asked politely.

"I'm a decorator. Right now I'm between jobs."

Sam slapped at his forehead. "Now why did I know you were going to say that." He looked around at the black-and-white furniture, the chrome and glass that seemed to be everywhere, disgust written all over his features.

"Your eyeballs really stand at attention in a room like this. I find it cold and austere. What happened to all my grandmother's things? The antiques in particular. I guess black and white is *in* this year," Sara said.

"Actually, black and white *is* in. I like things that are clean and crisp. Jon said he likes what I've done. Your grandmother's things were placed in storage. I made sure to catalog everything. How do you like the way your rooms turned out?"

Hard-Hearted Hannah answered for all of them. "Actually," she said drawing out the word the way Alexandra had, "we pretty much think they stink. We've been hanging out in Cisco's room. Is it time to eat?"

"No, it isn't time to eat," Jonathan snapped. "We're having cocktails because there's something I want to talk to all of you about. The least you could have done is dress for dinner. The three of you look like homeless people."

"Let's get to it, Dad," Sam said, marching into the sterile-looking living room. "Are these sofas leather or plastic?" he demanded.

Alexandra's chiseled features registered horror. "Leather, of course."

"They kill animals for leather. I'm not sitting on this stuff," Hannah said, dropping to the floor and crossing her legs. Her siblings joined her. "How long is this going to take? When are we going to eat?"

"As long as it takes, that's how long," their father snapped again.

Jonathan walked over to the bar, where he poured champagne into fragile flutes. "What's your GPA this semester?"

"Three-point-eight," the triplets said in unison. Their father looked pleased as he handed out the glasses.

"We all have high IQs," Sara said. "What's yours?" she asked Alexandra.

"It's gotta be single-digit," Sam muttered under his breath.

Jonathan cleared his throat. "Alexandra and I wanted you to be the first to know that we're getting married on New Year's Day. Of course we'd like you to attend the small formal wedding here at the apartment. To a long life rich with happiness," he said to Alexandra, a sappy look of adoration on his face. The triplets merely held the flutes but didn't drink from them or give any sign that they accepted the toast.

"Will Cisco be here for the wedding?" Sara asked.

"I rather doubt it," her father responded.

"Then count us out. Isn't it time to eat? By the way, we decided to drive back to school after dinner. We'd like to get the issue of Christmas cleared up now, though. We're going to spend the holidays with Cisco, Sam said."

"I closed up the house. You can't go there. Alexandra and I want you to come here so we can spend Christmas together. I have several parties planned. We're going to have a wonderful big tree. I want you here," he said coldly.

Sam's eyes narrowed, his slim body going tense. "We'll just open the house back up. I know how to turn everything on." His expression clearly defied his father to argue with him.

"We've always spent Christmas with

Cisco. Even before Mom died, we spent Christmas in the mountains. It's a tradition, and we aren't giving it up . . . Dad," Hannah said.

"Why don't we just grab a sandwich and head on back," Sam said, leaping to his feet.

"Good idea," Hannah said.

"I'm with you guys," Sara said, reaching for her brother's hand so he could pull her to her feet.

"You'll do no such thing. Oh, there's Maureen now, signaling that dinner is ready," Jonathan said, relief ringing in his voice.

"We're acting like spoiled ten-year-olds," Sam whispered in Sara's ear as they walked to the dining room.

Sara snorted. "That's exactly how I feel right now. Alexandra has Gold Digger plastered right across her forehead. This dinner is going to tell us the tale. If there aren't six chairs at that table, I'm leaving. You know what else, I'm never coming back, either."

Cisco always sat at the head of the table, their father and Sam at her right, Hannah and Sara on her left. There were six chairs, Sara saw to her relief. Now, the big question was, who was going to sit in their grandmother's chair, or would it remain empty throughout the meal?

The chair at the head of the table remained empty as Jonathan took his seat next to Alexandra.

Sara stared at her brother through the tulip arrangement and over the top of the huge thirty-five-pound turkey. She gave a slight nod. Within seconds, Sam had moved his plate and chair to the opposite side of the table and was seated alongside his sisters.

The blessing was short and curt, offered up by Jonathan. Cisco always blessed and thanked God for a full ten minutes before she carved the turkey.

Sara continued to watch Alexandra through the tulip arrangement as her father nervously picked up the carving knife. She tried to be objective about her father's choice in women but found it hard going. Cisco always said to look for the good in people. That was even harder to do.

Alexandra was dressed to perfection in designer wear, hair coiffed so that not a strand was out of place, makeup so flawless it looked like it had been sprayed on. Eyes bluer than a summer day couldn't be real. Her teeth were small and pearl-like. They glistened behind glistening lips. Diamonds winked in her ears, on her neck, her wrists, and her fingers. She looked *shellacked*. Sara's final assessment was that Alexandra was as vapid and artificial as a Barbie doll.

Her new stepmother.

Like hell.

Sara felt kicks to both her ankles. They were so in tune with each other, she knew she wouldn't have to tell Hannah and Sam what her assessment was of Alexandra. She knew they were thinking exactly what she was thinking.

"When is Cisco going to be able to leave that place you stuck her in, Dad?" Sam asked.

"When the doctors say she can leave. I don't think that's going to be anytime soon if that's your next question."

"You know what I think, Dad. I think we might need a second opinion," Hannah said as she chomped down on a celery stick. Alexandra winced delicately at the loud crunching sound.

Jonathan Cisco laid his carving utensils on the side of the platter. "Okay, I've had enough of this. Things are what they are, and they can't be changed. I'm a lot older and wiser than you are. I know what's best, and that's all I'm trying to do. I'm sorry you don't like the way things are going. You might as well know right now, I'm going to be making some changes in the company. You probably won't like those either. Now can we just eat this damn dinner?"

Sam reared back in his chair. "What kind of changes? The three of us are stockholders, or did you forget that? You can't make changes unless Cisco and the three of us agree. For now, we don't agree. Of course, that might change when we know what you're planning. Do you want to tell us now?"

"What's gotten into the three of you? Why are you being so obnoxious?"

"You know damn well why, so don't pretend you don't. Did Cisco tell you she gave us her stock on our last birthday? Nope. I can see by the look on your face she forgot to mention that to you. We have the controlling interest, Dad," Sara said.

"I think this might be a good time to leave," Hannah said, pushing her chair back. "Before things turn ugly." Sara and Sam moved in sync.

At the doorway to the stark-looking dining room, the trio turned. "It was so nice to meet you, Alexandra." Out of the corner of her mouth, Sara said, "Now!"

Jonathan Cisco watched, his face turning white, when three folded sheets of paper, the promise lists, sailed in his direction. "All bets are off," Sam said, turning on his heel.

"You didn't tell me your children were

such little shits, Jonathan," the Barbie doll said.

"She called us little shits," Sam said.

"We *are* little shits. Cisco would be appalled at our manners. She brought us up better than this. Get your stuff together and let's get out of here. What I said back there about not returning here . . . I meant it," Sara said as she brushed a tear from the corner of her eye.

Outside, in the cold, brisk November air, the triplets linked arms. "I'm starving," Sam said.

"You were born starved. There's a Burger King down the street and around the corner. You wanna go for it?"

Over Whoppers, fries, and milk shakes, they discussed the day's events. "What's he going to do when he finds out you lied, Sara? I'm talking about the company shares," Sam said, biting into his Whopper.

"God only knows. I had to do something. I just felt I had to do it for Cisco. We're going to call her as soon as we get in the car. I know she'll go along with it. Let's just hope she has her hearing aid in and answers the phone. Did either one of you like our future stepmother even a little bit?" Sara said, sucking on the straw in her milk shake.

Hannah stopped chewing long enough to respond. "No, not even a little bit. Dad likes her enough to be marrying her, so maybe he sees something we don't. If we were younger, she'd be the wicked stepmother and sending us off to boarding school. That's my take on Alexandra."

"Sam, you're a guy, what does Dad see in her?"

"The outside of her. Dad always went for looks. She looks good standing next to him. That's what men want. Remember how pretty Mom was? But she was pretty in a motherly, wholesome way, not like that artificial bunny. Single-digit IQ is on the money. I bet she *excels* in counting money, though," Sam said as he wadded up his napkin. "I gotta say this is probably the worst Thanksgiving we ever had."

"Christmas is going to be great. Let's just hold on to that thought. This is just a little rough patch in the road," Sara said as she cleared the table. "If we get you back to school on time, Sam, you might be able to take that little exchange student you've been drooling over skiing tomorrow."

# 2

~ · ~ · ~

*L*oretta Cisco knew it was the Trips on the phone the moment it rang. She always thought of her grandchildren as the Trips. She fiddled with the small hearing aid in her right ear, making sure the volume would enable her to hear every word her beloved grandchildren uttered. She hoped she sounded more upbeat than she felt. Frederica, Freddie for short, her loyal golden retriever, squirmed next to her on the sofa until her head was in Cisco's lap. She listened, too.

"It's us," the triplets bellowed in unison. "Crank up your hearing aid, Cisco, because we're in the car heading back to school."

"So soon! Good heavens, what time was dinner? I thought you weren't leaving till tomorrow." They all started to jabber at once. "One at a time, please," their grandmother pleaded.

"We crashed and burned, Cisco," Sara said. "Dinner was scheduled for three o'clock. We ate at Burger King at three-forty-five. It wasn't all that bad, and now we're on our way back to school. You should have let us spend Thanksgiving with you."

"It was awful," Hannah chimed in.

"The pits," Sam said. "You're gonna hate the apartment. They redecorated everything but your room. Black and white is in this year. We slept in your room last night. It still smells like you."

"They're getting married New Year's Day. We passed on the invite," Sara said. "Dad got a little pissy when we told him we were spending Christmas with you. He said he closed up the house." They started to babble again.

Freddie barked, then Cisco said, "Slow down, one at a time."

"We're never going back there, Christmas or wedding, whatever. Just this minute we decided instead of going back to school, we're heading your way. Too bad we listened to you, Cisco. We could all have been together right now. We should arrive sometime late tonight. Keep the light burning," Hannah said.

The old lady smiled as her left hand stroked the golden retriever next to her. How she loved those rambunctious grandchildren of hers.

"The best part is we're taking the next semester off so we can take care of you. We're gonna spring you out of that place you're in over Christmas break. Don't tell anyone, though. Oh, another thing, Cisco, we told Dad a lie. We said you gave us your stock on our last birthday. You might have to back us up on that, or we're all gonna be sucking wind. He wants to change things at the company. You will back us up, won't you?" Sam asked, his voice sounding anxious, his eyes on the road ahead of him.

"Good Lord! What else did you do? We'll discuss your last semester later." A smile played around Cisco's mouth as she listened to her grandchildren's excited voices. Freddie was sitting up, aware that something was, as Cisco put it, going down.

Cisco leaned back and listened to the tale her grandchildren were spinning for her. She heard them, but her thoughts were on their pending arrival in a few hours. When they finally hung up thirty minutes later, she started to cry. Freddie leaned into her, licking her wet, wrinkled cheeks. She blubbered then because there was no one to see or hear her but Freddie. "Get me some tissues, baby," she said.

Freddie returned, dragging the toilet tissue from the bathroom. She barked as she nosed the long trail of paper into Cisco's hand. "No tissues, huh? For what this place costs you'd think there would be linen hankies everywhere." Freddie was back on her lap, nudging the toilet tissue into a pile in her mistress's lap.

"I'm glad they're coming, but I hate for them to see me in this god-awful place. I hate it. I hate that Jonathan put me here. This is what happens when you get old, Freddie. They don't want you anymore. They just want to hide you away and forget about you. Then they try to ease their conscience by showing up for ten minutes on a holiday. *If* they show up at all." She started to cry again, as her memories took over.

She allowed fifteen minutes for feeling sorry for herself. *Goddamn it, I'm not feeble and I'm not feebleminded either. I might be having a temporary setback with my cataracts and hearing aids, but I'm not ready to bite the dust yet. And I sure as hell am not ready* for a place like this.

*A place like this.* It was a pricey establishment. She should know, she'd donated enough money to the facility over the years. With each generous donation she'd thanked God that she didn't have to live in such an institution. That's probably how Jonathan was able to slap her in there on such short notice, her being such a loyal contributor and all. She couldn't help but wonder what else he'd promised the company that owned Laurel Hills.

She'd been here once before, years earlier, taking the tour after a successful fund-raiser. The grounds were luxurious, full of mountain laurel, the state flower. The shrubs were manicured, the rolling hills, emerald green. And that's where the beauty stopped. The assisted-living quarters were three tiny rooms, bedroom, sitting room, bath, and a kitchenette. Everything was stainless steel and bolted to the floor so that residents didn't trip over anything. The floors defied description, tiles with some kind of tread on them. There were no paintings on the walls, no colorful cushions, no knickknacks of any kind. It was up to the patient to supply those things with the staff's approval. She hadn't brought a thing other than her clothes and Freddie.

She supposed she was treated well. A doctor came by twice a day. Four times a day her phone rang, and an anonymous voice on the other end asked if she was all right. A nurse showed up to help her shower even though she could do it herself. They brought food that at times was edible and other times not so edible. She had a television that she could listen to as well as books on tape. An aide walked Freddie five times a day.

She hated Laurel Hills.

But the Trips were coming. She clapped her hands in glee. One way or another, they'd make things right. Suddenly, her stainless-steel environment didn't seem as bad as it had before their phone call. Freddie squirmed and wiggled closer. Cisco hugged her tightly. As long as she had Freddie, she could handle anything.

Well, almost anything.

The Trips would handle the rest.

Alexandra Prentice watched her fiancé pace the long living room. From time to time he smacked his clenched fist into his open palm. She had to play it just right. She walked into the dining room, fixed two plates of food, and carried them into the kitchen. "Maureen," she said sweetly, "I'd like you to start a fire in the living room and set up a little table. Mr. Cisco and I will be dining in front of the fire. I fixed our plates, so all you have to do is warm them up. Oh, and don't forget the wine."

She went back into the living room. Jonathan was still pacing. She bristled at the fact that he didn't seem to realize she was in the room. If there was one thing she hated, it was to be ignored. Especially when she'd paid a fortune for her Escada ensemble. The little shits hadn't even been impressed with the way she looked. Compared to their jeans and Penn State sweatshirts, she looked like royalty. A tiara would have been a nice touch.

Jonathan continued to march up and down the room, only by then he was muttering to himself. He was oblivious to the fact that Maureen had sparked the fire and set up a small table with two spindly chairs. The wine bucket was set up, the table decorated with a fine linen cloth and a small arrangement of tulips. The dishes, silver, and glassware were Cisco's finest. When the housekeeper nodded, Alexandra walked over to her soon-to-be husband and touched his arm gently. He looked up in surprise.

"Darling, don't take this to heart. Your children were upset because . . . because they aren't used to change. They wanted their grandmother here, and that's understandable. I wish now that you hadn't invited me or made our wonderful announcement. It was too much for them to accept all at once. I know you feel as terrible as I do about what happened. Tomorrow is another day, darling, and we'll do double time working this out so that everyone is happy." Her voice was soft, almost a purr of intimacy, as she led him over to the table. "We have so much to be thankful for, Jon. It's Thanksgiving, so let's try to enjoy our dinner."

Jonathan looked first at the fire, then at the little cozy table, and finally up at the woman he was planning on marrying. He wondered if he was making a mistake. She smiled then. "I want to apologize for calling your children little shits. It was a bad moment. One I will regret forever. And, another thing, darling, I really wish you'd call your mother and wish her a Happy Thanksgiving. She's all alone."

Jonathan nodded. "You always know exactly the right thing to say, Lexy," he said, using his pet name for her. "Whatever did I do to deserve you? You're right, we have to work at making this come out right, and I will call Mom after dinner. I feel so bad about all of this. Did I ever tell you about the time Mom and the triplets . . . ?"

Alexandra smiled until she thought her face would split wide open. One tale led to another and then another until Jon was almost crying with despair. Like she really gave two hoots in hell about the past. She played the game, though. It was a good thing she'd been the one to set up the rules.

"Have some more wine, darling." If she kept plying him with wine, he'd soon forget his intention to call the old bat and possibly even the triplets to see if they arrived safely back at school. She wondered if it was true that the old woman had given her shares of stock to the triplets. Why would they lie? Why indeed?

It was one-thirty in the morning when Sam steered the black Range Rover up the winding road that led to a small gatehouse and security gate. Tiny dots of light could be seen on the other side of the gate. Roadway lights to guide late-night callers, he supposed.

"We're here to see Loretta Cisco," Sam said irritably. "What's the problem?"

"The problem is, *sir*," the guard said just as irritably, "we close and lock the gates at eleven o'clock. That means no one goes in or out unless they have a pass."

"Well guess what? They didn't mail us the pass card yet," Sara said.

Hard-Hearted Hannah rolled down her window in the back and poked her head out. "I thought this was an assisted-living facility, not a prison. C'mon, give us a break and open the gates. We're tired, and it's cold. Our grandmother has been waiting for us, and it is Thanksgiving. Call the office if you don't believe us, and let us in," Hannah pleaded.

"I just work here. I don't make the rules. I'm sorry, I'm not authorized to open the gates, and your name isn't on the list. You'll have to come back in the morning."

"Let me see that list!" Hannah said, snatching it out of the guard's hands. She took the pencil off the clipboard and scribbled their names. "Now we're all on your list. Okay, Sam, *HIT IT!*"

"Oh, shit!" Sara squealed, as Sam backed up and gunned the Rover in preparation for plowing down the gates.

"Best thing I ever bought was the brush guard for this baby. Cisco was so impressed when I told her this vehicle could do anything, even mow down some security gate. Who knew?" he quipped, his voice as shaky as his hands gripping the steering wheel.

Sirens wailed through the quiet night as floodlights sprang up, lighting the grounds in a bright orange glow.

"This probably wasn't one of our brightest ideas," Sam said as he tore down the gravel roads. "Don't be surprised if our asses get hauled off to jail."

"There it is, Building 16. Cisco's rooms are on the left. C'mon, c'mon, we need to see her before we get hauled off," Sara said, leaping from the Rover even before it came to a full stop. She could hear Freddie barking. She grinned as she ran up the walk and hurtled through the door. "We're here, Cisco!"

The old lady laughed. "I knew it as soon as I heard the sirens. Freddie knew it, too. The three of you come here and give me a big hug. Lord, I've missed you," Cisco said, standing up so her grandchildren could wrap their arms around her, careful not to disturb the soft cast on her arm. Freddie danced around in circles, waiting for her turn to be hugged. Sam was the first to drop to the floor to tussle with the golden dog, who yipped and pawed the young man.

"We plowed down the gate, Cisco. They said we weren't on the list. I wrote our names on the list of visitors. You did say you left a permanent visitation form for us, didn't you?" Hannah asked uneasily.

"I certainly did. Being a holiday and all, it's possible there's a relief guard at the gatehouse, and he didn't know. It's also entirely possible your father rescinded the pass," Cisco said. "Shhh, someone's coming."

The knock was loud and forceful, a nononsense sound. Sara opened the door. Standing in front of her were a Pennsylvania state trooper and three of Laurel Hill's security guards. Two nurses and a young man in a white lab coat brought up the rear.

Bedlam ensued as Freddie raced to the door, her lips peeling back from her teeth.

Her tail dropped between her legs as her big body quivered. "Easy, girl, easy," Sara said softly.

"Let's hear it," the trooper said, his hand on his holster.

The triplets started to talk at once. They played the game they'd always played, talking over one another, one finishing the other's sentence until the person they were talking to gave up and walked away. The trooper didn't budge. His hand stayed on his holster. Freddie continued to growl.

"It's one o'clock in the morning," a nurse with wiry gray hair said indignantly. "You've managed to wake up the whole facility. Our patients need their rest."

"The gate's a shambles," one of the security guards said out of the corner of his mouth.

"We'll pay for it," Sara said quietly.

"Yes, you will pay for it. I have to take you in," the trooper said. "You can make arrangements with the judge in the morning. Then again, if he's off hunting because this is a holiday weekend, you'll have to wait till Monday morning. Let's go."

The triplets ran to Cisco and hugged her. "We'll be back. You aren't mad at us, are you?"

"Good Lord, no. This is the most excitement I've had in the last six months. Don't worry, I'll get someone to post your bail. Try to stay out of trouble. Was it a mind bender when that ugly gate went down?" she asked gleefully. "Did your adrenaline soar out of control?"

"The thrill of a lifetime." Sam grinned. "It was just like Tom Cruise in *Mission Impossible*, or was it *White Line Fever*? Whatever, it was a great feeling, and the Rover doesn't have a dent in it."

"Okay, macho man, let's go," the trooper said, leading Sam and his sisters out to the patrol car sitting in front of Building 16. "Get in," he barked.

"You don't have to get ugly about it," Hannah snarled. "We just wanted to see our grandmother. We have every reason to believe she's not being treated well here. We wanted the element of surprise to be on our side in order to make an accurate assessment of the situation. We're willing to pay for the gate."

"And was she?"

"Was she what?" Hannah snarled again.

"Mistreated?"

"I don't know. You got there right after we did. She didn't look too good to me in the little time I had to observe her. What do you guys think?"

"Not good," Sam said.

"Definitely not herself," Sara said. "Look, is it really necessary to arrest us?"

"You broke the law. Yes, it's necessary. What are you, triplets?"

"Why do you want to know?" Hannah snorted.

"My grandmother donated two wings to this place. She's not going to like your hauling us to jail. We both know that the people that own the place are not going to sign a complaint against us, so why are you putting us through this?" Sara demanded.

"Because you broke the law. Now, sit there and be quiet. You get one phone call when we get to the station. Consider yourself lucky that I don't handcuff the three of you."

The Trips looked at each other.

At the station, the trooper signed them in, then shoved a black desk phone toward Sam.

"Unless you guys know someone who has money to post our bail, it's Dad who gets the call." Hannah and Sara nodded miserably. Sam dialed. When Alexandra picked up the phone he mouthed her name to his siblings. "I'd like to speak to my father, Alexandra. Well, wake him up, this is important. Actually, it's very important. I realize what's important to me might not be important to him. Let me put it to you this way. My sisters and I have just been arrested. We need Dad to post our bail so we can get out of jail." His eyes were desperate when he looked at Sara and Hannah. "You'll tell him when he wakes up! Thanks for nothing. We won't forget this, Alexandra. You never want to piss the three of us off at the same time. Remember that, too."

"Looks like we're here for the night," Sam said, hanging up the phone. He turned to Hannah. "The next time you get a brilliant idea like that, keep it to yourself."

The trooper herded them along, down a long hallway to a small room with a rough table, four chairs, and a dirty two-way mirror. "I'll send someone in to take your statement."

"Hold it! Hold it!" a voice shouted from the hallway. "I'm here to post bail!"

"And you are . . . who?" the trooper queried, his jaw setting angrily.

"Mrs. Cisco's physical therapist. Finley Cooper."

Sam frowned. He knew that name from somewhere. He stared at the physical therapist, but his facial features didn't ring any bells. Like his sister, he shrugged.

"Mrs. Cisco asked me to post bail for her

grandchildren." He pulled a wad of bills big enough to choke a buffalo out of his bag.

Forty-five minutes later, after a phone call to a very vexed county judge who just happened to love Cisco candies, the triplets exited the station behind Cisco's therapist. They thanked him profusely as he led them to his car, where they piled into the backseat. The ride to the assisted-living facility was made in total silence.

They thanked the therapist profusely again when they climbed out of his car. Sara took a moment longer than her brother and sister. She bit down on her lower lip. "My grandmother doesn't belong here. We disagree with our father's decision to put her here. I just want you to know, and feel free to tell anyone on the staff, that we're going to get her out of here. One way or another."

"Look, I'm just a therapist here. I don't get involved in family disputes. Plus, I'm just here on a temporary basis filling in until the New Year, when my buddy gets back from his wedding cruise. If you have a beef or a complaint, take it up with the administration. Another thing, bailing out spoiled rich kids doesn't fall under my job description."

"Which spoiled rich kids are you talking about? We aren't spoiled, and we aren't rich. Our grandmother might be rich, but we sure as hell aren't. We go to college on academic scholarships we earned, and we all have part-time jobs. We support ourselves. If you have a problem with that, send us a bill, and we'll compensate you for the trip to town to bail us out. If you're an example of who's taking care of our grandmother, then we have a right to be worried. Good night, Finley Cooper, temporary physical therapist," Sara snapped.

"Guess you told him," Hannah said. "He's kind of cute in an angry sort of way. Let's go, I'm freezing."

This time, their greeting with their grandmother was more subdued. Freddie, though, was just as wired and wanted to play.

"Knocking down that gate was not exactly a wise thing to do," Cisco said. "Your father isn't going to take kindly to the report, and trust me, there will be a report," she said wearily.

"*Miz* Alexandra wouldn't wake up Dad when we called to ask him to post our bail," Sam said through tight lips. "That makes three stupid things we did in a little over a day. Walking out on good old Dad, plowing down the gate, and getting arrested. He'll fry our asses over this."

"Get off it, Sam. We're of age. All he can do is yell at us. He does that anyway, so what makes this time any different?" Hannah demanded.

"I don't know, it just feels different for some reason. The stakes are higher. In case you haven't been listening, this is serious business for a change," Sam said.

"It's late," Cisco said. "We have to think about sleeping arrangements."

"It's okay, Cisco. We have sleeping bags in the Rover. We'll tuck you in, then grab some sleep ourselves. Are you glad we came?" Sara asked anxiously.

"I'm so glad you came I don't have the words to tell you. I sat here all day feeling sorry for myself thinking about all of you at your father's. You're here now, that's all that matters. You don't have to tuck me in, but you can kiss me good night. Freddie and I have a routine we go through, and if I want it to work for us both, then we have to do it religiously."

When the door to the bedroom closed behind their grandmother, Hannah looked around and hissed, "This is one ugly place. I'm glad Cisco can't see what it looks like. The word *institutional* would be too kind. It smells like an institution, too."

"Let's leave it all for tomorrow. I'm knocked out," Sam said. "I'll get the sleeping bags. If you two get any more brilliant ideas, don't include me in them."

"What's with him?" Hannah demanded.

"I think guys get a little pissy when they get hauled off to jail. It does something to their psyche. You notice, we just rolled with it," Sara said.

"It was exciting, wasn't it?"

"Yeah." Sara giggled. "You really think Finley, the physical therapist, was cute?"

"Nah, I just said that," Hannah said, dodging a videotape that Sara sailed across the room in her direction.

"Maybe we shouldn't have thrown those lists at him as we walked out of the dining room," Sara said. "I'm thinking that was pretty childish on our part."

"By the way," Sam said, returning with the sleeping bags, "I remembered. Finley was an Olympic skier. That's why his name sounded familiar. He blew out both his knees. Never skied again."

"That has to be pretty rough, giving up an Olympic dream," Hannah said.

Thirty minutes later, they were settled for the night, snug in their respective down sleeping bags.

Sara turned until she was on her stomach and said, "When . . ."

Hannah, so in tune with her siblings, jumped in and finished what Sara was about to say. "When he didn't show up for our high school graduation, that's when it all went downhill. He was too busy entertaining Bambi what's her name. A trio of valedictorians, a first in the school's history, wasn't important enough to him to show up. It was all downhill after that," Hannah said.

"We can't unring the bell, so let's just go to sleep, okay? Tomorrow's another day. We can get up with the chickens and beat it to death then," Sara said, rolling back over before she curled up in her sleeping bag. "Night."

"Night," her siblings echoed.

From the bedroom, they all heard a soft woof.

# 3
~ • ~ • ~

*H*e was in that delicious place in sleep, half-awake, half-asleep, as he struggled to recapture the dream. His leg stretched out, certain it would touch Lexy's silky leg. Good thing? Bad thing? He wanted the dream back. Better not to think about Lexy. He squeezed his eyes shut and was immediately transported back in time to the happy place in his dream. A place that was tranquil and beautiful, with wonderful, loving people.

"We're ready, Dad," the triplets called, their gear piled up next to the car. He looked up to see his mother standing in the doorway. God in heaven, what would he have done without her when Margie died? What would the triplets have done without Cisco? She was the glue that had kept them all together. She never complained, never had a cross word for any of them. She'd stepped right in after the tragedy, and their lives never missed a beat.

He stared at her a moment later, loving the gentleness and strength of character he saw on her face. She smiled, a smile that always made his world right side up. It was a smile that said, we can do this together. She was beaming now, her cheeks pink with excitement for all of them. Even from where he was standing he could see the sparkle in her eyes. Sometimes he wondered why he was so surprised at her abilities. She'd risen from the ashes when his father died way too early in life. With very little money in the bank, a skimpy insurance policy, she'd started to make candy in the kitchen after she worked all day at the telephone company. It was a mother-son operation. She made the caramels and taffy, and he wrapped them when they cooled down. Then on Saturday mornings, they delivered them to all the stores in the area.

It took three years before his mother decided to go the catalog route with gift boxes of candies for the holidays. Another two years expanding the cottage at the foot of the Allegheny Mountains, and they were off and running.

"We'll bring you a present," the Trips shouted.

"I can't wait to see what it is. No dead fish now!" Cisco laughed.

"You guys sure you didn't forget anything?" he asked, climbing behind the wheel.

"Nope. We packed *everything*. Let's go, Dad!"

This was their first camping trip since Margie died. In one way he was looking forward to it, and in another way he was dreading it. The two-hour ride up the mountain had always included sing-alongs, jokes, and storytelling. He didn't know if he could pull it off with the same gusto as Margie had. He was going to try like hell. Maybe, though, they needed to change things. Not that he wanted to forget his wife; nor did he want his children to forget her. The past belongs in the past, he told himself.

Hard-Hearted Hannah brought it front and center. Twelve years old, and she knew exactly what he was thinking. "Let's talk about things. Let's make promises we will never break. Okay, Dad?"

"Well, sure. What do you want to talk about?" he asked as he steered the car up the winding roads, the scent of evergreens wafting through the open windows.

"Boys!" Sara and Hannah squealed.

"Girls!" Sam bellowed.

The questions came faster than bullets.

"When can we shave our legs?"

"How can we get the curl out of our hair?"

"When can we get our ears pierced?"

"What if a girl hits me? Hard?"

"How am I supposed to carry her books and mine, too, and still stand up straight?"

Earth-shattering questions they already knew the answers to because Cisco had made sure they knew. Cisco never left things hanging. He knew they knew about reproduction and all the womanly things they were supposed to know. Sam knew what he was supposed to know, too, because Cisco left nothing to chance. They were testing him, pure and simple. His answers took up the first hour of the drive, with the Trips giggling and laughing at his discomfort.

He knew he'd passed when Sam said, "Okay, now, let's get to the promises. You can go first, Dad, because you're the authority figure. Any promises we make today, we have to honor forever and ever. Is it a deal?"

"Of course it's a deal," he said happily. "A promise should never be broken. A man or a woman is only as good as his or her word. I want you all to remember that. Since I'm going first, here's what I would like you to promise me. I want your promise that you will never knowingly do anything to shame your grandmother, me, or yourselves. Whatever you undertake in life, I want you to give a hundred percent and no skimping anywhere along the way."

"We promise," the Trips said in unison.

"Good. I promise the same thing."

"Can we promise always to spend Christmas together? It was Mom's favorite time of the year, and she said she didn't care about other holidays, but everyone had to be home for Christmas," Hannah asked, a catch in her voice.

"That's a really good promise. I promise," Jonathan said.

"We do, too."

"I have a question before the promise," Sam said. "What will happen if . . . if something happens to Cisco? Will you get married again? What if we don't like who you're going to marry?"

Jonathan cleared his throat. "Nothing's going to happen to Cisco for a very long time." He hoped he spoke the truth. "We'll go on, though, if something does, just the way we did when your mom died. We'll stick together because we're a family. Family is the most important thing in the world. I promise you that I will not marry anyone you don't like. I would never do something like that to you. I want you all to stop reading those wicked stepmother stories. Do you hear me?"

"We hear you," they bellowed.

"Promise us that we can always stay with Cisco. Promise us that we'll take care of her if she gets sick."

Jonathan nodded. "That's an easy promise."

"I'm going to write all this down when we get back home, and we'll each get a copy," Sara said. "We have to save this list of promises forever and ever, okay, Dad?"

"You bet. They're all wonderful promises. They'll be easy to honor."

The balance of the trip was filled with other promises.

"Promise we can date when we turn sixteen."

"Promise we get to drive every weekend when we get our licenses."

"Promise three trips a year to New York and to Mom's grave in Metuchen."

And then the best promise of all. "Let's all promise to love each other the way Mom loved us and not let anyone or anything ever come between us."

Jonathan laughed. It was such an easy promise to make. He pulled the car to the side of the road and came to a full stop. He turned to look at his children and smiled as he plopped his hand down on the back of the headrest. Six hands slapped down on top of his. His left hand was the last to complete the tower. This was the Trips's way of sealing the deal.

Fishing, hiking, swimming, campfires, storytelling, sharing memories. It was going to be a wonderful five days.

The sound of the telephone woke him from his dream. He groaned and rolled over, his eye going to the caller ID next to the phone. He rolled back over. He didn't want to talk to Alexandra at five-fifteen in the morning. He didn't want to talk to *anyone* at five-fifteen in the morning.

Today was supposed to be a nothing day. A day just to stay in, possibly watch some videos, go out to dinner, or even brave some of the stores on Fifth Avenue. He hated shopping with Alexandra.

He knew he wasn't going to be able to get back to sleep. He might as well get up and have some coffee.

His head started to pound when he swung his legs over the side of the bed. Damn, how much wine had he guzzled last night? Obviously a lot, since he hadn't felt like this since shortly after Margie died. Back then, he drank just to be able to sleep. Sometimes it helped the gut-wrenching hurt, and other times it just left him feeling numb. He probably would have turned into an alcoholic if Cisco hadn't stepped in and straightened him out.

On his way to the bathroom, he stopped long enough to stare down at the zebra-covered chaise lounge. He wondered if he'd ever sit in it. He took two more steps before he saw the folded papers the Trips had tossed at him. Their copies of the promise list they'd made long ago. Just the sight of them made his head pound harder. Almost as hard as his heart was pounding. He'd deal with those later. Much later.

In the bathroom, taped to the mirror, was a note from Alexandra. He thought his head was going to spiral right off his neck when he read it.

*Darling, your son called late last evening just as I was leaving. I tried waking you but you were sleeping too soundly. Too much wine, darling. He said he needed you to bail him and his sisters out of jail. It seems they were arrested. I don't know where they are because he didn't say. He was rather surly but I guess that's understandable considering his predicament. I tried calling you when I got home but you didn't answer the phone. He was terribly upset. Much love, Alexandra.*

Jonathan sat down on the edge of the Jacuzzi. "Son of a bitch! Arrested!"

Twenty minutes later he was shaved, dressed, and in the kitchen, the telephone in his hand. It wasn't until an hour later, when he had nothing to show for all the calls that he had made, that he realized all he had to do was scroll back the caller ID, and the number Sam called from would pop up. He raced into the bedroom. The only call that came in after seven-thirty was a number he didn't recognize. He looked down at the note Alexandra had left him. She'd said she tried to call after she got home. Her number wasn't there. Was that because she hadn't left a message? *Damn, I can't think straight this morning.*

He gulped some more aspirin before he called the number on the caller ID. He felt light-headed when he heard the words, "Laurel Hills Police. Sergeant Lomax speaking."

Jonathan identified himself and stated his reason for calling. "Can you connect me with the arresting officer?" Damn, the Trips said they were heading back to school, and instead they'd gone to Laurel Hills to see Cisco. He listened, his shoulders sagging. He thanked the desk sergeant before hanging up. He needed to think. *How in the hell did it come to this?*

*How?*

The Laurel Hills Assisted Living Facility came to life at five-thirty in the morning. The triplets woke the moment the front door opened, bringing a cold draft swirling into the room. They looked up to see a cranky-looking nurse and an aide who looked even crankier. The nurse peered down at the three young people, and said, "Overnight guests are not permitted. We have rules here."

Hannah was about to tell her what she could do with her rules when Cisco appeared with Freddie. "It was a bit of an emergency," Cisco said apologetically.

"C'mon, dog," the aide said, yanking Freddie on the leash that Cisco was holding on to. Sam was unzipped and on his feet in a heartbeat, pulling Freddie's leash out of the aide's hand. "I'll walk her."

"Suit yourself. Walking dogs at this hour of the day isn't my cup of tea."

"I hate this place," Hannah said, beating at the sleeping bag with her closed fists.

"All right, Loretta, let's take our shower. And let's not be difficult this morning. I had a bad night last night with all that went on around here," the nurse said snidely.

"I'll tell you what," Sara said. "My sister and I will help our grandmother. You can go now and recover from your bad evening. Like right now," Sara added, her voice ringing with cold steel. Hannah was on her feet and holding the door open.

"This is irregular and will have to go on report," the nurse blustered.

"Oh, well," Sara said.

When the door closed behind the nurse, Cisco laughed. "I wish I had the guts to do that. She's a real curmudgeon."

"Do you need help when you shower?"

"No, actually, I don't. I have a waterproof sleeve that fits over my cast. I know where everything is. I'd like to be able to take a shower without someone watching me. Thanks, girls."

"Take your time. Yell if you need us," Sara said.

When the door closed behind Cisco, Hannah looked at her sister. "I hate even thinking this, but do you think once we leave, the people at this place are going to take their anger out on Cisco? We haven't been the ideal visitors, if you catch my drift."

"I was wondering the same thing. The long and short answer is, I don't know."

Sam and Freddie sailed into the room just as the phone rang.

The Trips looked at one another. They mouthed the word, "Dad," at the same time.

No one made a move to pick up the phone.

"He's just going to keep calling," Sam said. He played with Freddie's leash, swinging it one way and then the other before he looped it over the doorknob.

The phone continued to ring. They all ignored it. Finally, it stopped ringing.

"We can stay till Sunday afternoon, but we're going to have to go to a motel if the rules say we can't sleep here. Once Cisco is asleep, we can leave and be back here by five-thirty when she wakes up. We need to make some kind of plan. There must be a dozen motels in the area, so that's not going to be a problem," Sara said.

Hannah looked around the tiny apartment. "This place looks worse in the daylight than in the dark. Oh, look, Freddie is waiting outside the bathroom door. Thank God for that dog's devotion. Listen, let's take Cisco out today. I say we head for town and get that second opinion we were talking about. Since this is a holiday weekend, doctors might not be too busy. I'll call the AMA and see if they can recommend a good eye surgeon. What do you say, gang?"

"Let's go for it," Sam said. "There goes that pesky phone again."

The cranky nurse with the wiry gray hair

barged into the apartment, a breakfast tray in her hands. "Answer the phone!" she ordered.

"We don't want to," Sam said. His tone clearly said she better not want to either.

"Smart-ass," the nurse said under her breath. "Is she still in there?" She gestured to the bathroom.

"Yes, she's still in there," Sara said.

The phone stopped ringing just as Cisco appeared, fully dressed, her hair brushed back into a tight bun at the nape of her neck, a rosy glow to her features. She looked wonderful.

"I brought your breakfast, Mrs. Cisco," the nurse said as she prepared to set it up.

"Oh. What is it?"

Sam lifted the dome off the plate and frowned. "It looks to me like a cold scrambled egg." He touched the yellow glob with his index finger. "Yep, a cold scrambled egg. Four cooked prunes. You hate prunes, Cisco. One slice of . . . yep, cold toast. Some kind of spread on top of the toast that leads me to believe it's artificial. A cup of coffee. Now, why did I know it was going to be cold, too. A packet of powder for cream and one sugar packet. I wouldn't eat this. Would you guys eat it?" he asked his sisters.

"Nope."

"Let's see if Freddie's interested." Sam set the plate on the floor. Freddie sniffed it, looked up at Sam as though to say, "you're kidding, right?" She walked away.

"We'll be going out to breakfast," Hannah said, picking up the plate.

"Cisco, how does blueberry pancakes, eggs over easy, crisp bacon, hot toast, warm syrup, soft butter, and fresh-squeezed orange juice sound? Not to mention pots of *hot* coffee, " Sara asked.

The phone started to ring again. The cranky nurse looked like she was about to pick it up, but Sam's scowl stopped her.

"You can't take patients away from the premises unless the guest has a pass. All the office personnel are off for the holiday, so no passes can be issued. These matters have to be taken care of in advance. We have rules!"

"Oh, well! I guess we'll leave it to you to explain when the office personnel get back. We're going out!"

"You can't do that! We have rules. They're for the patient's benefit," the cranky nurse grumbled.

"I'm sure they are, but we're just going to ignore those rules for now," Hannah said.

A knock sounded on the door before it opened cautiously. A young girl, a volunteer by the look of her uniform, stuck her head in the door, and said, "Mr. Cisco called and said he's been calling his mother and there's no answer. He wants to know if something is wrong. He's on hold. What should I tell him?"

Hard-Hearted Hannah marched over to the door. Her voice was syrupy-sweet when she said, "Tell Mr. Cisco the Trips have the situation under control."

Sara held the door open for the nurse, who was carrying the breakfast tray. "We won't be needing you anymore today, Nurse. We'll be back at some point. I'm just not sure when that will be exactly. You have a real nice day now," she added as she shut the door.

Cisco clapped her hands. "Oh, you don't know how I've wanted to do that. Thank you."

"You know, Cisco, part of this is your own fault. You should have called us. We would have dropped everything and come here. I know, I know, you don't whine, and you don't complain. But there are exceptions to everything, and this is one of those times when you should have made an exception," Sam said.

The phone rang again. The Trips looked at one another. Hannah nodded as she picked up the receiver. "This is Hannah Cisco speaking. How may I help you?" She made a face as she held the phone away from her ear to listen to her father's tirade. She waited until her father paused to take a deep breath before she spoke. "I think the question should be, what's gotten into you, Dad, not the other way around. You washed your hands of us, remember? You got yourself a new life. We prefer the life we've always had. Mom must be spinning in her grave at what's going on. No, I'm not going to let you speak to Cisco. Not after what you did to her. Sara, Sam, and I are going to make this right. Our arrest? Cisco took care of it for us since you couldn't be reached. We can take care of ourselves. I don't hear you saying you're rushing here to check things out. We are not screwups!"

Sam snatched the phone out of his sister's hand. "Listen, *Pop*, your squeeze said you were sleeping and couldn't be disturbed. She said she'd tell you in the morning. I'm just damn glad it wasn't a life-or-death matter. Stop pretending you care. I know what you care about, and it isn't us, or Cisco. You're just trying to make yourself feel better. You told us a man or a woman is only as good as their word. You also said a promise is something to be honored and never taken lightly. The three of us talked about that, and, you know what? Those were *Mom's* words. You just repeated them. Mom was always as good as her word, and she never, ever broke a promise. You have a nice day now."

"Wow!" Sara said.

"Oh dear, now your father is going to be upset," Cisco murmured.

"That's a good thing," Hannah said. "Maybe he'll finally wake up to what's going on. We didn't want you to worry about us, Cisco."

Cisco made her way to the couch and sat down. "He really hurt you three, didn't he? You led me to believe everything was all right between you and your father. Why didn't you tell me how unhappy you were?"

The Trips clustered around her. "At first we thought he was just working too hard and didn't have time for us. As you know, it all started when he didn't show up at our high school graduation. That was his way of telling us we were on our own. He was going to start living his own life. A set of teenage triplets didn't help his image," Sara said.

"When we'd ask to go to New York, he

would always say it was a bad time. I guess it was because of his different girlfriends. We called, he was never there. He never called. As you know, holidays were the only time we saw him. We just gave up. You never said anything either, Cisco. We all just sucked up the hurt. It's not that we begrudged Dad a life of his own. He was there every step of the way after Mom died, just the way you were, Cisco. He took what we consider a wrong turn on the road. Who knows what he thinks. Come on, this is getting us nowhere. Let's just go out and have a nice, productive day," Sam said, reaching for Freddie's leash.

There wasn't a happy face in the group as they trooped out to the Rover. Except maybe Freddie, who loved to ride shotgun. She yipped her pleasure, dancing around Sam's feet until they finally arrived at the car.

Jonathan Cisco stared at the phone for a long time. The headache was still pounding away at the base of his skull. He looked around the new modern kitchen, hating it. He missed the old wooden table with the claw feet and the chairs with the red-checkered cushions. Cisco's rocking chair that she'd kept in the corner by the pantry was gone, too. In the past, she'd sit in it, rocking contentedly while she waited for a pie to bake or a stew to finish simmering.

She'd never really liked the apartment, though, preferring to live back in her cottage in the mountains.

He tried to clear his throat. The last time he felt this bad was the day of Margie's funeral. A part of his life had died that day. Another part of his life died yesterday when the Trips tossed what they called the promise list at his feet.

Head pounding, he made his way through the apartment to his mother's bedroom. Inside, with the door closed, he went straight to the old-fashioned dresser filled with photographs. He picked up a picture of Margie smiling into the camera. He remembered the day it was taken. They'd picnicked at the lake, played Frisbee, eaten too much, canoed, and rolled around on the spiky grass. When the sun set, and the temperature dropped, they'd built a fire and toasted weenies and marshmallows. Margie had looked up at him, and said, "Even when they grow up and leave us, we'll still worry about them. We'll be forever parents."

Margie would have been a forever parent. He'd dropped the ball. His eyes burned unbearably as his fingers traced the outline of his wife's face. God, how he'd loved her. Even now, just looking at her picture, he could feel a stabbing pain in his chest.

Jon sat down on the edge of the bed, aware suddenly of his mother's scent. The Trips always made a point of saying she smelled wonderful, just the way a grandmother was supposed to smell. Margie had had a special scent, too. There were times when he had literally felt drunk just being in her presence.

Margie would not approve of what was going on in his life. Margie with the laughing eyes. Margie who only saw good, never bad. Like his mother, she'd been the wind beneath his wings. Everything she did and said during those wonderful, far-too-short years, was an indication of her love for him. And the Trips, of course.

She always packed him a lunch even though he could afford to buy it on the outside in those early days of their marriage. He never knew until later that the reason she discouraged him from buying his lunch was so she could put notes in from the girls and always one from herself, too. Sometimes they would be silly little notes, sometimes serious, always loving. He'd never wanted to give that up. More often than not if there was a client in town, Margie would pack a picnic basket.

She ironed his shirts, too, saying no Chinese laundry was going to take care of her husband. She saw to every side of him, the physical, the mental, and the spiritual. Margie was all things. God, how he'd loved her. How he missed her.

No, Margie would not approve of Alexandra. She would say she was shallow, all facade and no substance. Margie would have stayed in the cottage with Cisco, seeing to her wants and needs until it was time for cataract surgery. She would not tolerate what was happening between him and the Trips. Not for a second. He could hear her now. "You make it right, Jon, and you make it right, now." If Margie were here, alive and well, none of this would be going on. He'd stepped off the path and gotten lost.

An unforgivable sin. One that hopefully could be rectified.

He didn't stop to think; he barreled out of the room in search of his car keys and heavy jacket. He swallowed a handful of aspirin before he headed for the elevator. Maybe he could still make it right.

Maybe. Such a little word for such a monstrous problem.

# 4

~ . ~ . ~

Larkspur, a small residential town nestled in the foothills of the Allegheny Mountains, had one claim to fame—a small, private, top-notch hospital staffed with Pennsylvania's best doctors, surgeons, and nurses. The Trips eyed the pink brick structure with the stately columns by the front entrance before Sam swerved the Range Rover off the main road to follow a winding brick road to the main entrance of Larkspur Community Hospital. "You guys go in. I'll park and take Freddie for a long walk. Run up the flag if you need me."

"Why are we here?" Cisco asked nervously, as Hannah helped her down from the car.

"We're getting a second opinion on your eyes if we can, Cisco. Our thinking is the hospital won't be busy the day after Thanksgiving, and we might luck out and be able to get you an appointment with a good doctor. Just think of it as another checkup. By the way, when was the last time you had a medical checkup? Why did you wait so long once your sight started to go?"

"I waited because Harry Nathan said I had to wait. I had shadowy vision and could get around, so it wasn't really a problem. Harry said the cataracts had to be ripe before they could be removed. My last checkup was cursory at best, but to answer your question, it was done when Jonathan brought me to Laurel Hills. Jonathan said Harry Nathan was too old to be practicing medicine and couldn't see any better than I could. They did tell me my arm was healing nicely. The therapy helped a lot. The soft cast comes off in three weeks. When you're older like me, your bones take longer to heal." Her voice sounded so sad, Hannah and Sara cringed.

"We're more interested in your cataracts than we are in your bones, Cisco. I just wish you had told us how bad your eyesight was," Sara said gently. "Look, this might not even work. It seems these days you need to make appointments months in advance. I look at it this way: Nothing ventured, nothing gained."

"I didn't want you to worry. When you get old and you say you're starting to fall apart, you tend to believe it. If you don't talk about it, it doesn't seem so bad. Then there's the fear factor. You are absolutely right, nothing ventured, nothing gained," Cisco said smartly.

They had reached the lobby, and ushered Cisco to a seat next to a luscious-looking ficus tree. The furniture was tasteful as well as comfortable. Seasonal paintings of the famous mountains decorated the walls. The carpeting and drapes covering the plate glass windows were lightly tinted with restful colors that were easy on the eyes. An enormous fish tank with colorful tropical fish covered one entire wall. All in all, it was a homey, comfortable lobby.

A small reception area was manned by a pretty young girl with a ponytail tied with a bright yellow ribbon. She smiled as Hannah approached the desk.

Sara sat down on a chair next to Cisco and picked up a magazine. She looked up when a tall man with a shock of red hair stood over her. "You're one of the triplets, right?"

"I beg your pardon," Sara said stiffly. Her first thought was that the authorities were closing in on them for hijacking Cisco. She almost swooned with relief when she didn't see a state trooper behind the tall man.

"Joel Wineberg," the man said, holding out his hand. "My sister Clair belongs to your sorority. We met during your fundraiser last year at Penn State. I'm sorry to say I don't remember which one you are, though. You and your sister are identical as I recall."

Sara pointed to Hannah at the reception desk. "I'm Sara. Yes, I remember you. I also remember your robust donation. I hope we thanked you properly for that. You're a pediatrician, right? It's nice to see you again. Do you work here?"

"Raising money for elder hospices is at the top of my priority list. I was happy to make the donation, and, yes, the sorority sent me a glowing letter of thanks. To answer your question, I'm on staff. Are you visiting someone? Can I help?"

"You know what, maybe you can help us." She leaned over to Cisco. "I'll just be a minute." Cisco nodded, as Sara walked a short distance away, the pediatrician at her side. She quickly explained why they were there. "Is there an ophthalmologist on call today? We only have till Sunday to make arrangements, then we have to head back to school for finals."

"This is really your lucky day. Zack Kelly

is on duty. All of us single guys gave the married doctors the weekend off so they could spend it with their families. Zack turned down twenty-seven hospitals to come here. When I tell you he's the best of the best, believe it. Your instincts were right on about this being a slow day. Let me see what I can do."

"Okay, I appreciate it. Thanks."

Hannah wiggled her eyebrows when she rejoined Sara and Cisco. "We're here five minutes, and you're hitting on some guy. Let's get real here. This isn't going to work. You need an appointment. The hospital is shorthanded because of the holiday. I made an appointment for the week after Christmas. The doctor's name is Zack Kelly. That child over there," she said, pointing to the girl behind the reception desk, "said Dr. Kelly was a hottie." She wiggled her eyebrows again.

"What's a hottie?" Cisco asked.

"A super good-looking guy who has everything going for him," Hannah replied, laughing. "Who was that guy you were talk-ing to, Sara?"

"Clair Wineberg's brother Joel. Don't you remember, we met him at the sorority fund-raiser last year? He gave us a real healthy donation. He's on staff here. Right now, he's trying to get Dr. Zack Kelly to take a look at Cisco. It's all in *whom* you know," she said airily.

Thirty minutes later, a nurse with a crinkly smile and twinkling eyes ap-proached them, pushing a wheelchair. "Mrs. Cisco, Dr. Kelly will see you now. Dr. Wineberg said the rest of you should go to lunch and come back at three o'clock. Dr. Kelly is personally going to run some tests on your grandmother and will make his evaluation. Is that all right with you?"

"Don't we have to sign her in or . . . or something?" Sara asked.

"I can handle all that, Sara," Cisco said. I have my medical cards. I've done this be-fore. Run along and do what the nurse said."

"And we all know who Mrs. Cisco is. We

sell her boxed candies in the gift shop. They're one of our best sellers. Scat now," she said, waving her arms toward the door.

"Cisco, is . . . are you okay with this?"

"Of course I'm all right with this. Explain to Freddie, she'll understand. Here, give her my scarf. She'll curl up with it till I get back." The girls hugged her, their eyes wet.

"She told us to go," Hannah said, sitting down.

"Since when did we ever do anything someone else told us to?" Sara responded, sitting down next to her sister.

"I think this is one of those times when we should do what we're told," Hannah said, getting back up. "Look, there's Sam and Freddie at the door. Tell me we did the right thing here."

"We did the right thing," Sara assured her sister, walking to the door. She opened it, Cisco's scarf dangling from her hand. Freddie threw back her head and howled.

"It's okay, girl, she's coming back. We're coming back. We have our marching orders," Hannah said, filling her brother in on what was happening. "Are you okay with it, Sam?"

"I'm not important. Is Cisco okay with it?"

"Yeah. Yeah, she is."

"Then let's go to lunch."

Jonathan Cisco heard his name being called as he blasted through the lobby, but he didn't turn around. When the call became more shrill, he did turn because some of the early-morning tenants were staring at him.

"Jon, where on earth are you going so early in the morning? I thought . . . we did say we were going to spend the day together, didn't we?" Alexandra Prentice asked breathlessly.

His step slowed so she could catch up to him. As always, he was struck by her beauty. "Yes. No, I'm going to have to take a rain check, Lexy. I have to go to Pennsylvania. Why didn't you wake me last night? I didn't get your note till this morning."

"Darling, I did try to wake you. I did

everything but douse you with ice water. Actually, I did think about upending the ice bucket but thought better of it. If you're going to Pennsylvania, I'm going with you. I think we should talk about it first, though. Rushing off like this without a plan could backfire. You don't want that, do you?"

She was right, of course. "All right, let's go around the corner and get a cup of coffee."

Alexandra linked her arm with his as they walked out of the building and around the corner. She hated steamy little coffee shops because she invariably ended up smelling like whatever they were cooking. Jon loved the cozy atmosphere and the early-morning bustle. She particularly hated the thick mugs coffee was served in and the plates with the cracks going down the middle. Cups and saucers of fine china were required to drink her gourmet coffee. She detested paper napkins, preferring fine linen. When they were married, these early-morning excursions to local coffee shops would come to a screeching halt.

She sensed that something had happened between the time she'd left Jon's apartment last night and her meeting him minutes ago. Something serious, something Jon wasn't going to share with her. It was probably some damn, noble, family thing. Whatever it was, he was going to have to get over it. Fast.

"Now tell me what happened. Two heads are better than one, darling. Let's see if we can make some sense out of whatever it is that's bothering you. Please don't tell me it's those tacky, childish lists the children threw at you."

He bristled at her words. "That's part of it," Jonathan said. His voice sounded defensive to his ears. "Sam plowed down the gates at Laurel Hills with his Range Rover. The guards called the troopers, and they were taken to the station. My mother managed to post their bail. I'm sure I can get the administrator to drop the charges.

"What's really worrying me is they took their grandmother out of the facility. I don't know where they took her or if they plan on taking her back. For all I know they could be on a plane bound for Europe. I'm sure she's safe with them. They would never do anything to hurt their grandmother."

*I should be so lucky*, Alexandra thought. "Darling, why do you always jump to the worst possible conclusion? The children probably took your mother for an outing. Yes, they are thoughtless; yes, they are acting childishly, even infantile. They're spoiled rotten, Jonathan, and you know it. It's their way or no way. How did you let that happen? They didn't show you one iota of respect yesterday. Forget about how brutal they were to me. You're their father, they owe you respect."

"The Trips aren't like that at all, Alexandra. Cisco and I brought them up to be independent. They think for themselves. Their first loyalty is to their grandmother, and I can't fault them for that. They feel like I let them down, and I did. I regret that," Jonathan said miserably.

"Good heavens, Jonathan, they're acting

like snotty little vigilantes. They thumb their noses at you, and you still defend them. I just don't understand that kind of thinking. You did everything you could. You made sure your mother was taken care of. How can that be wrong? Just because they think like the children they are doesn't make what you did wrong. You would never forgive yourself if something happened to your mother, and I understand that. Now, what is it you want to do? Whatever it is, I'm behind you a hundred percent. Just know this, darling, you can find out everything you need to know and get the same results on the telephone as you would by traveling six hours ." Alexandra reached across the table to take his hand and squeeze it.

"I guess I'm overreacting. You're right about the trip versus the calls."

"I know I'm right," Alexandra purred. "If there's one thing we should both know for certain, it's that your mother is safe with your children. I'm just as certain as you are that they won't let anything happen to her.

They're probably all having the time of their lives while you sit here stewing and fretting over their antics."

It all sounded good and plausible, and yet something nagged at him. How easily he could be swayed. He forced a smile he was far from feeling.

"Now, that's the Jonathan I know and love," Alexandra trilled.

It was two o'clock when the Trips returned to the Larkspur Community Hospital. They agreed to take turns staying in the car with Freddie. Hannah took the first shift.

"You know what I notice about this place?" Sam said.

"No, what?"

"The smell. Remember when Ben Foster broke his leg hang gliding, and we visited him almost every day at the hospital?" Sara nodded. "Well, this place doesn't smell like that. You know, disinfectant, alcohol, brewing coffee, and all those other awful smells. This place smells like . . . vanilla and oranges. Kind of like Cisco's kitchen when we were little and she was whipping up all those different-flavored caramels for the holidays."

"You're right, it does. What do you think they're going to say, Sam?"

"I don't know. I wish I did. Do you believe even for one minute that Dad stuck Cisco in that place for all the right reasons?" Sara shook her head. "He's going to be pissed to the teeth when Cisco doesn't go back."

Sara looked at him sharply. "We *have* to take her back to Laurel Hills, Sam. Cisco has to stay there till we break for the holidays. It's just for a few weeks. We also have to think about Freddie. We can't take her to the sorority house, and you can't take her to your frat house either. Cisco will die without Freddie, and we all know Freddie has never been separated from her. I don't see what other choice we have."

Sam slumped in the chair he was sitting in. He wished he was a kid again so he could run to his safe haven—the tree house in the old maple. It was where he and his sisters ran to hide and cry when things piled too high on their shoulders. They'd even slept there after their mother died. His eyes started to burn. What was going to happen to all of them? A family was supposed to pull together, not fall apart the way theirs was doing. Cisco was in fragile condition right now, their father was off the deep end with his latest girlfriend and now they had to cope and try to make things right for their family. As the immediate man of the family, he had to soothe his sister's raw emotions. And his own. The sudden burning in his eyes made him bite down on his lower lip.

He risked a glance at Sara. Even though she was the oldest and sometimes the bossiest, she was also the most loving and sensitive of the three. He knew she was hurting now. His arm reached out. She squirmed closer. They sat in an uneasy silence as they waited.

From time to time, Hannah could be seen walking Freddie past the main entrance, Cisco's scarf tied around her neck.

At seven minutes past three, a family of four opened the wide double doors to the main lobby. Freddie jerked free of Hannah's hold on the leash and barreled through the lobby and down the hall, Cisco's scarf flying in the wild breeze she created. Sara and Sam gave chase just as the elevator door swished open to reveal Dr. Joel Wineberg and a man wearing a Stetson and a Harley Davidson sweatshirt. Freddie barked, then growled, which meant, Get out of my way. The family of four stood aside, their eyes on Freddie and what she was going to do next. No one was surprised when she threw back her head and howled.

Hannah skidded to a stop and went down on one knee as she finally grabbed Freddie's leash. "Gotcha!" she said breathlessly, looking up with wide-eyed wonder at the tall man in the Stetson.

"Yes, of course I'll marry you. When? Which one are you?" The tall man grinned.

"Great! Two weeks from Sunday. I'm Hannah. And you are?"

"The man who's going to marry you," he quipped.

Hannah laughed. "Mom always said the man of my dreams would show up when I least expected it." She held out her hand so he could pull her to her feet. Freddie continued to howl.

"Nice scarf," the guy in the Stetson said, fingering the messy stitching on the wool scarf draped around Freddie's neck.

Her hold on Freddie secure, Hannah said, "I made it for my grandmother when I was thirteen and just learning how to knit."

"I'm impressed. You must have used some good yarn." He had laughing eyes that crinkled up at the corners. "My God, you really do all look alike!" he said in stunned amazement.

Hannah's head bobbed up and down. "I'm sorry about Freddie. She wants to see my grandmother."

"I think we can arrange that," Joel Wineberg said. He waved his arms, palms upward. "The Cisco triplets." He waved his hand at the man standing next to him. "Dr. Zack Kelly."

"Sara," Sara said, holding out her hand. She blinked. This scruffy-looking guy couldn't be the highly regarded ophthalmologist, Dr. Zack Kelly.

"Hannah. I already said that, didn't I? I can't let loose of Freddie to shake your hand." *Oh, God, this is Cisco's doctor!*

"Some other time, okay?" Zack Kelly grinned, his eyebrows wiggling a là Groucho Marx. "Hopefully, before we get married."

Hannah's face turned so red she could feel the heat radiating outward.

"Sam," Sam said, giving the doctor a bone-crushing handshake.

"Why don't we go outside and talk. It's not that cold, and Freddie can stay with us," Dr. Wineberg said.

They trooped out through the lobby and then to the benches under the overhang.

"Well?" Sara said, fixing her gaze on Joel Wineberg even though Zack Kelly was the ophthalmologist.

Dr. Kelly cleared his throat before he pushed his Stetson farther back on his head to reveal a mass of ebony curls. He set aside his playful personality and turned professional. "I'd like to admit your grandmother for a few days. I ran a few preliminary tests, but there are a few more I'd like to do that will take longer than twenty-four hours. She is in good health. We had a long talk. She's amenable to checking in, but it seems Freddie's well-being is what will clinch the deal. I'd like to admit her as a new patient since she's . . . ah . . . *on the lam.* No sense looking for trouble. She's okay with that."

"How long will she have to be here?" Sara asked.

"That pretty much depends on your grandmother. This is a private hospital, so she can stay as long as she likes as long as she's willing to pay the portion of the daily charges that her insurance doesn't cover. She's all right with that, too. Again, Freddie is the stumbling block. Now, as to the cataracts. I could zap them off tomorrow, but

Monday would be better. They're more than ready to come off. It should have been done several months ago, but we won't go there. Your grandmother is amenable to having it done Monday morning. Before she makes a final decision, she said I had to talk with the three of you. So I'm talking."

"We have to leave for school on Sunday afternoon. We have finals," Hannah said, her face filled with worry. "I don't want her to have to go one day longer than she has to without seeing. Freddie's our big problem."

"I can stay till Tuesday afternoon," Sam said. "I have a final at eight A.M. Wednesday morning. I can study here as well as I could at the frat house. I'll find a motel that allows dogs. Worst-case scenario, we'll sleep in the Rover."

"I can come back down Tuesday night and stay till ten A.M. on Thursday. I'll have to drive like a bat out of hell to be back for a final at four P.M. I can do it. While I'm here I can pick out my wedding dress." Hannah grinned. Dr. Kelly turned pink.

"I can leave school Thursday afternoon and stay till Sunday," Sara said. "I think we've got it covered. Will she be able to return to the assisted-living facility that Sunday? She'll have to stay there until we can leave school for our Christmas break and get the house ready for her, at which point we'll take her home and stay with her. Does this work for everyone?"

Her siblings and the doctors nodded. "Then it's a go," Dr. Kelly said. "If you'll excuse me, my patient is waiting to hear the outcome of our little meeting. I signed her in as an outpatient, but she will have to be admitted. In the meantime, I'll have one of the aides bring her downstairs, and you can all go out for an early dinner. She needs to see her dog, and that dog needs to see her. Healing happens quicker when there's a loving animal in the picture. It was nice meeting you all."

"I'm being paged," Dr. Wineberg said, looking down at his pager. "It was nice seeing you again, Sara. I'm glad I was able to help."

"Me, too. I don't know what we would have done without you."

The red-haired pediatrician looked at the three of them. "I have a feeling the three of you would have figured out something. I'll see you," he said, sprinting for the door.

Sam looked at the expression on his sisters' faces and burst out laughing. "I wish you could see yourselves. You look . . . so damn *sappy.*"

Hard-Hearted Hannah chopped at her brother's arm. "There's two of us and one of you, so watch it. You want to talk about sappy, what about Sonia, that exchange student you're tutoring in English? When you see her coming you do everything but roll over so she'll scratch your belly. Give up?"

"Yeah, okay," Sam snorted. He never won with the two of them. Never.

They didn't need to be told that their grandmother was coming down the hall. Freddie strained at her leash, slamming her body against the glass doors. She did everything but turn herself inside out the moment her beloved mistress came into sight.

The moment the door opened, and the nurse pushed the wheelchair through the opening, quicker than lightning, Freddie sprang free and was in Cisco's lap, lathering her with wet kisses.

Cisco squeezed Freddie so hard, the retriever yelped, but she didn't jump off Cisco's lap.

"I heard we're going out to an early dinner, and then it's back here for me. This is a good thing," she said, getting out of the wheelchair with the nurse's help. "They tell me the Red Circle Inn allows pets, so Freddie will be all right. This is so kind of you all to be doing this for me. That nice young doctor even called in an orthopedic man to check out my arm. They did an X ray, and he said the bone is healed. I just have to be careful. It's all so wonderful. I just feel like crying. It started out being a miserable, lonely holiday, and now it's beyond anything I could have hoped for."

Beaming with happiness, the Trips hugged

her. They led her to the car and settled her with Freddie on her lap before they all started to talk at once.

"How many times do I have to tell you, one at a time!" Cisco said. Tomorrow, even though it's Saturday, an audiologist is coming to check my hearing. Dr. Kelly didn't seem to think I had the right hearing aid. Now, wherever we go for dinner, let's make it someplace where I can pick up what I'm going to eat. I have a lot of different drops in my eyes, so now I can't even see shadows. Freddie needs something good to eat, too. You've been giving her water, haven't you?"

"Yes, to everything, Cisco," the Trips said in unison.

"You like Dr. Kelly then, huh?" Sam said.

"Very much. He explained everything to me in detail. He encouraged me to ask questions. Doctors never talk badly about other doctors, but I had the feeling he doesn't have much respect for Dr. Nathan, my doctor at home. Sometimes age and experience are blessings, and sometimes they aren't. Dr.

Kelly said they've made incredible strides in laser surgery. I will have to wear glasses, but I'll be able to see."

Suddenly Cisco's high mood plummeted. "We aren't going to tell your father, are we?"

"Absolutely not. We are going to call Laurel Hills and tell them you won't be back for . . . let's say, ten days to be on the safe side. We don't want Dad filing a missing persons report on you. I'll call the apartment and leave a message for him, too, just to be on the safe side," Sam said.

"Oh, I love it when you three come up with a plan that actually works. But I wish you had told me you were getting married, Hannah," Cisco teased.

Hannah's face turned red. "Oh, that . . . that . . . *doctor!*"

# 5
❧ · ❧ · ❧

*T*he Cisco corporate offices were in a loft over a warehouse on Hudson Street in downtown Manhattan. It wasn't the best address in town, but Cisco didn't care about such things. This was where they'd set up shop when the company became viable, and she'd refused to move, saying, "Why should I move to midtown and pay exorbitant rent to make someone's wallet fatter? Better my wallet should get fat." He hadn't argued the point because back then he'd believed his mother was an astute businesswoman and he'd agreed with everything she said.

It was Alexandra who pointed out that with more visibility, along with the Internet, the company would grow at the speed of light. Alexandra had also said they needed to hire younger, brighter people. Buttoned-up MBAs demanding high salaries and even higher expense accounts. New commercials needed to be made because it was time to put the old grandma and grandpa skits out to pasture where they belonged. Everyone, she said, knew when you got old, you had false teeth, and couldn't chew caramels and taffy. "Get real," Alexandra said so disdainfully that he'd felt inadequate for days.

How well he remembered the day he'd brought up Alexandra's ideas with Cisco. She'd looked at him like he'd sprouted a second head. She'd cut to the chase in a twinkling. "If it ain't broke, don't fix it." She'd gone on to say they paid their bills on time, the employees were happy, the buying public was happy, the Trips's trust funds were robust, as was his own. We have integrity, was her bottom line.

Jonathan climbed out of his car, aware suddenly that there were lights on in the offices. On a Sunday morning? Hattie, the office manager, the office *everything*, must have forgotten to turn them off on Wednesday when she left for the holiday weekend. Hattie was old; it was time for her to retire, just as it was time for John and Henry to retire. New blood was needed. New ideas, new packaging. Which brought him to his second question of the morning. *What the hell am I doing here? Why did I leave Alexandra sleeping snugly in my new bed to come here?* was his first question. He shrugged as he entered the warehouse and took the elevator to the office floor.

He was stunned to see Hattie, Henry, and John at their desks. They looked up as one, frowned, then went back to what they were doing.

"How's Loretta, Jonathan?" Hattie asked as she thumbed through a stack of invoices. "Tell her we miss her. What's wrong, Jonathan? You look a tad peaked to me." She sounded like she didn't care if he looked peaked or not, it was just something to say.

Jonathan's first reaction was to tell her exactly how he felt. These three, even the other office workers and the factory workers, were like family. No buttoned-up MBA would have dared to tell him he looked peaked or call the owner by her first name.

"What are you doing here?" he snapped.

"Working," Hattie snapped back. "Watch your tone, young man. You haven't been around much lately, or you would know demand is exceeding supply. You might want to think about going out to the factory and giving everyone a pep talk. Morale is down with Loretta being . . . it's just *down*. It's the Christmas season, and we're so far behind it's pitiful. That's what we're doing here on Sunday. We were here almost all day on Thanksgiving, Friday, and yesterday, too. In case you care.

"By the way, what happened to the plans for the Christmas party and the bonuses? I can't do everything, Jonathan. This place is going to hell! What *are* you doing here?"

It was a good question. *What the hell* am *I doing here?* "I came here to *think.*" Jonathan said, going into his cluttered office. He slammed the door. He sat down, his gaze going to the wall where a picture of the first shipment of caramels being loaded onto one of their delivery trucks hung. It was one of his favorite pictures.

The door opened. Hattie stood in the doorway. Jonathan sighed.

Hattie Dapper was as round as a pumpkin and just as colorful. She had snow-white hair and wore tiny little glasses; granny glasses, she called them. She sucked on caramels all day long. Sucked, not chewed. He wondered if Alexandra was right, and if Hattie had false teeth. He'd always been afraid to ask.

He loved Hattie. She had to be at least seventy, a few years younger than Cisco. She was a dynamo, single-handedly overseeing everything and making sure deadlines were met and things worked smoothly. She was mad now, her glasses jiggling on the end of her nose. She was also the Trips's god-mother, and as such she could say whatever she wanted, when she wanted. He knew he was going to get an earful at any second.

"What?" he barked.

"What? What? You know what, Jonathan. You're slacking is what. Ever since you started keeping company with that woman, things have gone downhill around here. That needs to stop. We need you here. Your mother needs to know you're doing your share. Don't think for one minute we don't know what's going on. We do. Another thing, the only reason, Henry, John, and I are still here is because of Loretta. Since you came here to *think*, let me give you some-thing to *think* about.

"That young woman you're seeing, the one you met in the health club . . . you said you met her when you were dripping sweat. Actually, you bragged about it to John. You told Henry she was decked out in a set of de-signer workout clothes and still managed to look ravishing. But she wasn't sweating. Do you know why she wasn't sweating, you dumb *galoot*? She was just at that health club to find herself a rich husband. You fell for it, too. You know how I know? Because I went there and pretended she was my niece. I got real chatty with one of the trainers. That's one of the perks of being old. Young people trust you, confide in you because . . . well, they just do. The trainer told me more than I wanted to know. She doesn't sweat! What does that tell you? She never went back once you swept her off her feet. I slipped the trainer fifty bucks to call me if she ever showed up again. I should have saved my money." The little woman grimaced as though she'd just bitten into a sour lemon.

"You did what?" Jonathan roared. "I'm on my last nerve here, Hattie, and you just stepped over the line. You and everyone else around here need to stop sticking your noses into my private business. I should fire all of you."

Hattie clucked her tongue. "What's stopping you, boy? You're going to do it after the first of the year anyway. If you want to fire us now, go ahead. Aside from not sweating, your girlfriend has a big mouth, too. You're moving the offices to midtown, you're going to retire all of us old-timers, and you're stepping into Loretta's shoes, an impossible feat, and not because they're women's shoes either. I'm ashamed of you, Jonathan Cisco, and I hope you can sleep at night. How *do* you look at yourself in the mirror? The people I really feel sorry for are your mother and the Trips. I'll leave you now so you can *think.*"

The minute the door closed behind Hattie, Jonathan's head started to ache. What he really wanted to do was bang his head on the desk in frustration. Why did everyone in his life feel compelled to stick their noses into his business? Why did everyone have a damn opinion where he was concerned?

Jonathan leaned back in the deep, comfortable swivel chair he'd broken in years before. If he moved to new offices in midtown, he'd have to get one of those ergonomic chairs and a shiny desk with a telephone system designed by some rocket scientist. He cringed inwardly.

He looked around at the clutter, at the business of running Cisco Candies. This worked. The chair worked. The desk held the family's life. It worked, too. The old black telephone worked just as well as shouting at the top of one's lungs. *If it ain't broke, don't fix it.*

Would there be room in midtown for all the family pictures dotting the walls? Would new customers, assuming there would be new customers, be offended by the pictures of the softball league the company sponsored? Alexandra said they would. Would they think all the pictures of the Trips sappy and maudlin? And what about Margie's picture? Would that have to go because she belonged to the past? He reached out and picked up a picture of his wife with her arms around the Trips. They were laughing uproariously as they prepared to go white-water rafting. Memories ran through his mind as his gaze swept the walls. His eyes burned when he remembered how Margie always knew when he was upset or tense about something. She'd knead his shoulders and neck, her slender fingers massaging and yet caressing those tense areas. When Margie was alive, he rarely got a headache. These days he went to bed with an aching head and woke up with his head pounding. He should think about buying stock in an aspirin company.

"I miss you," he whispered.

He thought again about those first weeks after she'd died, which had been so terrible. For him, for the Trips, for Cisco, too. They'd practically lived at the cemetery. They'd sent balloons up with little messages inside. Then Sam said he wanted to send a bottle down the creek with a message in it. They'd done that, too, when they returned to the mountains, because it made them all feel better. Then Cisco said enough was enough, and the daily visits had to stop. Not entirely, though. When they stayed in New York they went as a family once a month carrying flowers, sometimes just greenery with a ribbon attached. He went more often, he simply didn't tell his children or his mother about the visits. He knew the Trips went on the sly, too. They just didn't talk about it either.

His thumbs worked at the dust on the picture he was holding. "I'm getting married, Margie." He looked around, then up at the ceiling as though he expected his dead wife to materialize. "I meant to go to the cemetery to tell you. I swear, I meant to."

He tried to remember the last time he'd visited his wife's grave. *Years.*

Shame and guilt engulfed him. He hunkered into himself, his emotions running wild.

Jonathan set the picture back where it belonged on his desk and picked up the phone. He dialed the Laurel Hills Assisted Living Facility. Ten minutes later he hung up the phone, his heart thumping in his chest. His mother was still AWOL. The Trips's cell phone didn't respond to his calls, an eerie-sounding voice saying the customer he was trying to reach was out of calling range. Where were they?

"Hattie!" he bellowed.

"What?" she bellowed back.

"Come here!"

"I'm busy, *Mister Cisco.* Someone has to take care of business. You're just *thinking.*"

Hattie never called him Mister Cisco. Never. He needed to pay attention to these little things. He lumbered up out of his chair and walked out to her desk. "I need you to do something for me."

"Whatever it is, you'll have to do it yourself. I'm too busy, and I'm on my own time today just the way John and Henry are on their own time. What?"

"Sometimes you really are ugly, Hattie. I want these," he said, pulling the Trips's promise lists out of his wallet, "framed."

Hattie reached for the lists and opened one of them. For one intense moment, he thought Hattie was going to cry. Instead, she squared her plump shoulders, and said, "You broke every single one of these promises. I'm on *their* side. That means, do it yourself, *bubba!*"

Jonathan reached for the lists. "When did you turn so ugly?"

"The same time you did. I'm busy now. Go think some more."

"You're hateful, Hattie." He looked down the long room, to where John and Henry were sitting. They refused to look at him.

"I own this company. A little respect goes a long way."

"Your mother owns this company, and until some lawyer tells me differently, I report only to her. You have to *earn* respect," Hattie snapped. "You are dismissed, *Mister Cisco.*"

If he'd had a tail, it would have been between his legs as he slunk down the hall toward his mother's office. He opened the door and stepped in. Like her room at the apartment, it smelled like Cisco. It was neat and orderly, just the way she was.

He walked over to the old rolltop desk and felt something tug at his heart. All the little cubbies were filled. There was no dust. That had to mean Hattie cleaned the office. The green plants Cisco loved were healthy and vibrant. Hattie must water them, too. There was no dust on the pictures either.

The far wall was what Cisco called the family wall. She proudly showed it off to vendors and distributors as well as new customers. There was a story for every picture.

He looked down at the last two rows of pictures. Everyone was there but him. Four years' worth of pictures and not one of him. He thought his heart was going to leap right out of his chest. It was Cisco's way of telling him he didn't belong to the family anymore without saying the words aloud.

The sudden feeling of loss he experienced was so overwhelming, he thought he was going to black out.

Ten minutes later he was in his car. He had no destination in mind, knowing only that he didn't want to go back to the apartment. He didn't want to go over seating arrangements for his wedding dinner; nor did he want to discuss flowers and satin ribbons. He wanted to *think*.

Alexandra didn't sweat. Hattie had made it sound so profound. Was he just being a stupid, dumb male, or was sweating really important? His son, Sam, would probably know, but Sam didn't want to talk to him. Maybe he needed to test Hattie's theory by suggesting to Alexandra that they work out together.

Twenty minutes later he parked the car. Rockefeller Center. He and Margie used to bring the Trips here to ice-skate. Maybe he could get a latte, shift into neutral, and think. Before he exited the car, he dialed the Trips's cell phone number again. The same eerie voice said the customer he was calling was still out of calling range. Shoulders slumped, he locked the car and headed for the steps that would take him down to the ice-skating rink and more memories.

\* \* \*

They were gathered in the sunroom to say good-bye. It was an exceptional room, with its wide, panoramic view of the mountains that showed off the light dusting of snow that had fallen during the night. The trees and shrubs looked pretty, like the front of a Christmas card. The lighting inside was subdued, making everything seem warm and cozy. A gas fire burned brightly, more for atmosphere than warmth.

"I hate to leave, it's so warm and toasty here," Sara said.

"I wish you'd get a move on. If the temperature keeps dropping, the roads are going to freeze. I can hold the fort. Don't worry about us," Sam said. Freddie barked in agreement.

"Sam's right, girls, go now and be sure to call as soon as you arrive safe and sound."

"We will, Cisco," the girls said, as they hugged her and Freddie. "I'm so glad they allow dogs to visit here in this room. Joel told me this morning that they have pet day every Friday for the patients," Sara said.

"Will you just go already," Sam said with feigned exasperation. "And if you smack up my car, your ass is grass, Sara."

"Nag, nag, nag. Bye everyone. We'll call when we get home, and make sure you call us in the morning after Cisco's surgery. By the way, before I forget, Hannah called Laurel Hills and told them Cisco is with us enjoying a little holiday. She didn't offer up any additional details. She then called Dad's private number and spoke to Alexandra, who said Dad went out early this morning and has been gone all day. She said she didn't know where he went because he didn't leave a note. Hanny said Alexandra sounded like she was telling the truth. Anyway, Hanny told her Cisco was with us, and you were fine and dandy. End of call. Okay, okay, we're going." Another round of hugs and kisses ensued before they left the sunroom. Freddie hopped off Cisco's lap, her scarf trailing on the floor as she scampered to the door with them for one last good-bye.

"You take care of her now, girl," Hannah said, dropping to her knees to hug the retriever. She saw the boots, the jeans-clad legs, and groaned as she looked up at Dr. Zachary Kelly.

"I'm not wearing a cummerbund at the wedding," Zack Kelly said. He was grinning from ear to ear as he pushed back his Pittsburgh Pirates baseball cap.

Flushing, Hannah could only mumble, "Okay. What kind of hat are you planning to wear?" as Sara dragged her out the door and down the hall.

"I dreamed about that guy last night," Hannah said breathlessly. "He wasn't wearing a cummerbund at the wedding. What do you suppose that means, Sara?" she asked fretfully. "Oh, Freddie was the flower girl. She had a little silk pouch around her neck full of flower petals. I think it was a beautiful wedding. Do you think I'm losing my mind? He is *sooo* cute, though."

"It means . . . it means whatever you want it to mean. Damn, the roads are starting to ice up. I hope the interstate is okay. C'mon, shake it, Hanny."

"Well, I think I might like the dream to mean something," Hannah said, hopping into the Rover and buckling up. "You know what else, I think I'm going to knit him a scarf for Christmas. You know, for taking care of Cisco. That's a nice gesture, don't you think? Brownie points and all of that. If I start on it when we get back, I might be able to finish it before we take Cisco back to Laurel Hills. I'll wrap it up real pretty. Guys like stuff like that."

"Go for it then," Sara said, turning the car lights on.

"I think I will. I really think I will." Hannah settled in for the long drive back to school.

At ten minutes past ten the following morning, Dr. Zachary Kelly strode into the sunroom, his face wreathed in a wide smile. Sam and Freddie both jumped to their feet.

"Piece of cake, Sam. That's another way of

saying it went well. Your grandmother is doing fine. One of the nurses will come and get you when it's time for you to see her. Freddie can't leave this room. I'll make sure someone comes down to sit with her while you visit. You should call your sisters now. By the way, are they . . ."

Sam grinned. "No, they aren't seeing anyone. You have a clear, open field. You might want to pass the word on to Dr. Wineberg. If it means anything, I wouldn't wear a cummerbund either." He could hear the doctor laughing all the way down the hall. He waved as he slammed through the swinging doors that led to the surgery ward.

Sam gingerly lowered himself to the small sofa and patted his leg for Freddie to hop onto his lap. "She's okay, girl. She's okay. Before you know it, she'll be able to see you clearly. She's okay. Magic words, Freddie. I have to call Sara and Hanny now," he said, pulling out his cell phone. Freddie tugged at the scarf around her neck until she had it bunched into a ball. The golden dog lowered her head on top of the scarf and closed her eyes. She had understood everything Sam said. She could rest easy now.

The devil sparked in Sam's eyes when Hannah answered after only one ring. "Cisco's okay. Everything went well. I haven't seen her yet. Someone is going to stay with Freddie when it's time for me to visit her. I'll call you from her room so you and Sara can talk to her. Hey, Hanny, if you wash and wax the Rover for six weeks, I'll tell you what Zack said about you." He held the phone away from his ear when his sister started to squawk. "Okay, okay, you had your chance. Bye."

# 6

~ · ~ · ~

*T*hey were a miniparade, Dr. Kelly and Dr. Wineberg walking alongside Nurse Alice, who pushed Cisco's wheelchair down the hall to the main lobby, where Sara, Hannah and Freddie waited. Cisco, wearing wraparound dark glasses, held out her arms the minute the swinging door closed behind her wheelchair. The golden streak zipping toward her made her laugh aloud. "I missed you, too, sweet baby. Oh, you feel so good!" she said, hugging the golden retriever and smothering her with kisses. Freddie only stopped long enough to bark and bark in pure joy.

Alice pressed the button that opened the plate glass doors, and then they were outside in the biting air. She stopped, setting the brake on the chair so Cisco could stand up.

"I don't know how to thank all of you. I can send you bushels of candy, but that hardly seems enough for all you've done for me. Can I donate a room, a wing, something?"

"Can I just tell you one more time how thrilled and delighted I am that you, Alice," she said, reaching out to pat the nurse's hand, "and you two young men are going to spend Christmas Eve and Christmas Day with our family."

"The invitation is more than any of us expected. We'll be there with bells on," Zack said.

"Inviting us for Christmas is a pretty special thank-you," Joel Wineberg said. "Look, I have a tonsillectomy scheduled in a few minutes. I just wanted to say good-bye and to wish you well. It was nice meeting you all." He quickly offered his hand to everyone. "I'll see you Christmas Eve." His gaze lingered a minute longer on Sara before he sprinted off down the hall.

"You're good to go, Mrs. Cisco. If you have any problems, call me, day or night. Take care of your mistress, Freddie. It was nice meeting you all," Zack Kelly said, shaking hands all around. "As Joel said, we'll see you on Christmas Eve. I have a patient waiting. Take care," Dr. Kelly said, his tone professional, his expression just as professional.

A horn tapped lightly, as Sam swerved to the curb. Hannah stood rooted to the spot, a gaily wrapped package in her hand. Damn, he hadn't said one personal word to her. "Men stink," she muttered. She turned to the nurse and handed her the package. "Will you give this to Dr. Kelly?"

"Of course I will. It was nice meeting you all. Take care of yourself, Mrs. Cisco, and I'll see you on Christmas Eve. I'm working the early shift Christmas Eve, so I won't be able to drive with Dr. Kelly and Dr. Wineberg, but I will be there. We all get Christmas off this year, but we have to work New Year's so staff can be with their families. I'm really looking forward to spending a holiday with a real family. I know Dr. Kelly and Dr. Wineberg feel the same way. In fact"—she winked slyly—"it's all they talk about."

Freddie pawed at the nurse's leg. She bent down, tickled the retriever behind the ears, and smiled. "How does it feel to have your eyesight back, Mrs. Cisco?"

"There are no words to tell you how it feels. I think God gave me an early Christmas present. I can actually see. The snow is beautiful, just beautiful," Cisco said exuberantly as she looked around at everything before she climbed into the car. "Each day I see a little more clearly. The orthopedic doctor said I don't have to wear the soft cast any longer. I feel like I was just reborn. If you three hadn't stepped in, I'd still be languishing in that awful place. I love you so much."

"You're not supposed to cry, Cisco," Sam said gruffly.

"I'm not crying. Am I, Freddie? I think I

can handle anything from this moment on. Good-bye, Alice, thanks for everything." The nurse waved, a smile on her face.

"Before you can ask, her name is Alice Hampton and she's forty-one years old. She was my private nurse. She took wonderful care of me. And she's a dog lover like me. She reminds me of your mother. She's sweet and gentle, with a wonderful, soft touch. She's one of those nurses who really cares about her patients. Her husband was a firefighter who died in the line of duty ten years ago. She has no children, but she does have two Yorkies—Lily and Lennie. I told her to bring them on Christmas Eve. The more the merrier. I'm just so damn happy." The Trips laughed along with her.

"You okay with the game plan, Cisco?" Hannah asked.

"I'm very okay with it. You're dropping me off at Laurel Hills. You're turning around and heading back to school for the balance of your finals. Then you're packing up and coming back here to open up our house, after which you will return to Laurel Hills to spring me and take me home where I belong. Did I get all that right?"

"You're on the money, Cisco," Sam said. "Who's calling Dad?"

"I think I would like the pleasure of doing that if it's okay with the three of you."

Cisco smiled at their collective sigh. Her world was right side up.

The lounge was as comfortable as a doctor's lounge could be. Zack Kelly poured himself a cup of hazelnut-flavored coffee and carried it over to a recliner. He'd catnapped in that particular chair hundreds of times. He eyed the donuts in the colorful pink-and-white box.

"Don't even think about it! Those things will kill you," Joel Wineberg said as he flopped down in a chair across from his colleague. "So, what do you think?"

Zack grimaced. "I hate good-byes. I couldn't think of one damn flip thing to say. I really like her. I thought I was being clever with Mrs. Cisco when I asked her to talk about her family. You know what, she saw right through me and volunteered Hannah's whole life story. I felt like a sneak."

Joel laughed ruefully. "Hell, I can top that. I called my sister Clair and got the skinny on Sara from the day she joined the sorority. I think I have her life story, too. They're triplets," he said, his voice ringing in awe. "Think about this, if we marry them, and I'm not saying we will, we could each have a set of triplets. In a way it's kind of scary. They think like each other. They talk like each other. The brother is a guy. Brilliant observation right there. He's just like they are only he has a slight edge. He can *anticipate* us. It kind of spooks me if you know what I mean."

"I have their cell phone number," Zack said, his voice sounding jittery. He seemed less like a doctor and more like a young man in love.

"Oh, yeah?"

"Yeah."

"Maybe we can call them over the weekend. You know, just to say hello and ask about Mrs. Cisco. A generic kind of call," Joel said. "Of course we could find out just as easily by calling Mrs. Cisco herself."

"Mrs. Cisco said the three of them want to work in the business when they graduate. Their corporate offices and the candy factory are in New York. She did say she's thinking about closing up those offices and opening them up somewhere in this area. She said a lot of her employees are older, and she wants them close by because they're like a big family. I jumped right on that and encouraged her. There's some kind of problem with the father, but I don't know what it is. I didn't think it was any of my business, so we didn't get into it. Hate to drink and run, but I have a surgery scheduled in thirty minutes. Seems kind of dull around here without all of them. I really liked that dog."

"Yeah. Me, too. Don't lose that number."

Zack Kelly laughed. "Not a chance."

"It's only six o'clock, Jonathan, where are you going?" Hattie demanded.

"Don't worry about where I'm going, Hattie," Jonathan snapped. "I was in here at four o'clock this morning. If you want to stay, then stay. I'm going to work out, then I'm going home. You might not believe this, but I do work at home, too.

"Call for you, Jonathan," Mabel, the switchboard operator, shouted. "It's your mother!"

"You're kidding! Put her on the speaker-phone," Hattie bellowed. "We want to say hello." She enjoyed watching Jonathan roll his eyes.

"I'll take the call in my office," Jonathan said as he stomped his way back down the hall. His heart was beating so fast he thought he was going to pass out at any second. He tried taking great, deep, smooth breaths to calm himself. He eyed the dusty clock on his desk. Alexandra would pout all night long if he kept her waiting. His heart continued to slam against his rib cage. He tried to calm himself. When the red light glowed on the phone, he almost jumped out of his skin.

He tried to make his voice cheerful. "Hi, Mom. You had me really worried. Do you mind telling me where you've been? Where are you calling me from? You can't just take off like that and not let anyone know where you are."

"I'm fine, son, even though you didn't ask me how I am. I had some things to take care of, and the Trips helped me. I had my cataracts operated on. I can see very well now. I can also think a bit more clearly and see things I guess I didn't want to see or deal with. My arm has healed nicely, too. But to answer your question, I'm back at this place you stuck me in, but I'll be leaving soon to return home. You know, Jonathan, you didn't come to see me once in the three months I've been here. You called me twice. I've had a lot of time to think while I've been here and while I was recovering at the hospital last week. I made the decision to close the offices on Hudson Street and relocate them in Larkspur. We'll move the factory this year, too. I want my family, all those dear people who want to relocate, to come here with us. Those who don't want to come will be given generous severance packages. The company will pay all moving costs for our employees. I'm also going to sell the apartment."

"Mom, what's come over you? You can't just . . . do something like that. Think of the consequences."

"I have thought about them, Jonathan. I've had nothing to do these past three months but think. Cisco Candies is my company. I can do whatever I want with it. I just spoke to Hattie and the others. They're all behind me on this."

"Mom, this is not a good thing. You turned the company over to me. Changes need to be made. We need to move forward. Moving to some backwoods town isn't going to do it." He cringed at how desperate his voice sounded.

"That's a matter of opinion, dear. There's nothing on paper about my turning the company over to you. I wanted to see what you would do before I took that route. Think of it as a test that you failed. I've made my decision, so there's no point in discussing this any further. Have a wonderful holiday and congratulations on your upcoming wedding. It would have been nice, Jonathan, if you had told me you were getting married yourself. Instead, I had to find out from the Trips. I have to hang up now. Freddie wants to go for a walk. I am just so thrilled that I can actually walk her myself. When you get to be my age, son, it's the simple things that give the most pleasure. Good-bye, Jonathan."

His eyes blinded by tears, Jonathan's shoulders slumped.

He felt a hand on his shoulder and knew it was Hattie even though he hadn't heard her come into the room. He could smell the caramels she was sucking on. He waited for her to say something brash, even insulting. When she didn't, he looked up and saw only sadness in her eyes. She patted his shoulder again before she walked out of his office, closing the door quietly behind her.

A harsh sob caught in Jonathan's throat.

He looked around, desperately hoping to cope with what he was feeling. He reached for Margie's picture and brought it to his chest. "Tell me what to do. Help me." Like a picture behind a piece of glass was really going to tell him what to do, much less help him.

He looked around for his coat, then remembered he was already wearing it. He held Margie's picture like it was his lifeline. In the outer office, he stopped and looked around at Cisco's loyal employees. Never his. "Good night, everyone."

"Good night, Jonathan, have a nice evening," Hattie said.

"I'm going to try, Hattie. I'm going to try."

He drove uptown to the gym, where he was supposed to meet Alexandra. She was waiting, tapping her foot, a hundred taps to the minute. There was no welcoming smile, only irritation in her eyes. She waited for an explanation, and when none was forthcoming, she picked up her designer duffel, which probably held a designer towel and designer cosmetics, and stomped her way to an exercycle.

"What speed are you going to bike?" Jonathan called over his shoulder. "What's your pulse rate?"

Alexandra shot him another irritated look as she struggled to position her rump just right on the hard seat. She pedaled at a little under two miles an hour. Jonathan smirked at what he was seeing. He increased his speed on the StairMaster until sweat poured down his face. "You aren't sweating, Alexandra. It doesn't work if you don't sweat," he singsonged.

The hour workout was an exercise in futility as far as Alexandra was concerned. Jonathan felt calmer, more at peace after the strenuous workout.

"Time to shower," he said, wiping his face with his sweat towel.

"I think I'll wait till I get home to shower. I don't like going outside after a shower. I don't want to get sick with the holidays around the corner."

"Okay. Wait for me in the lobby. We need to talk."

Alexandra frowned as she picked up her bag, coat, and Jonathan's coat. The weight of his coat slapped against her leg. Something heavy was in the pocket. She reached in and withdrew the heavy silver frame with Margie's picture. For one incredible second she thought she was experiencing a brain freeze. Her eyes were speculative as she looked around at the part-time athletes chugging away at the different machinery. Too fat. Too bald. Too short. Too married. Too wrong. And, not one of them was giving her a first look, much less a second one. Obviously, she'd picked the wrong gym. She shoved the picture frame back where she'd found it.

On the walk back to the car, Jonathan said, "My mother called me today. She's back at Laurel Hills."

"How nice. Where has she been?"

Not how is she? Is she all right? Or, are *you* all right, Jonathan? *How could I have been so blind* and *stupid?*

"With the Trips. She had her cataracts operated on. She can see again. They also took the cast off her arm. She sounded wonderful. Right as rain, as a matter of fact. She wants to move the offices and factory to Larkspur. I didn't argue with her."

"The next thing you're going to tell me is your mother is going to sell the apartment." Alexandra's voice could have chilled milk. "Which then brings me to my next question—where are we going to live when we get married?"

"Now that you've brought up the subject, I think we should discuss postponing the wedding for a little while until I can settle things with my family."

Alexandra's eyes narrowed. "Jonathan, the invitations have been sent out. We paid deposits on everything. The tulips are coming from Holland. I can't cancel now. We locked in the time with the minister. My gown has been altered. We can't postpone it. People will say you . . . people will say you *dumped* me." She started to cry.

Jonathan wondered why he was unmoved by her tears. He jammed his hand into his pocket and found the picture of Margie. He almost swooned at the comforting feeling that washed over him.

"You can tell everyone you dumped me if that will make you feel better. I won't deny it. Since I'm the one who wrote the checks for everything, including your gown, don't worry if we lose the deposits."

"Oh, Jonathan," she said, dabbing at her eyes. "What happened to us? Everything was so perfect until . . . well, it was just perfect. It's our life, our marriage. Why are you letting other people have a voice in our affairs?"

"Because those other people are my family, and they have a right to voice their opinions. Do you understand what I'm saying, Alexandra? They're my family, and they have a right. I forgot about that for a little while." His hand inside his pocket closed over the silver frame again. How good it felt. How right.

"I'll drop you off at your apartment, Alexandra. I have a meeting I can't postpone any longer."

"Just like that, bam, you're dropping me off at my apartment? I thought we were going to dinner. Are you saying you don't want me to go back to the apartment with you? Well, Jonathan, what am I supposed to do? I suppose this means I have to spend Christmas by myself!" she screeched, the decibel level so high that Jonathan shuddered.

"Alexandra, you could go home and spend the holidays with your family. It's what people do." He'd wanted his voice to be gentle and soft. Instead it came out tough and firm. The words suddenly made him feel like his old self again. His grip on the silver frame in his pocket was so tense, his fingers cramped up.

"You are beyond hateful, Jonathan. Don't bother dropping me off. I don't want you going out of your way. I'll take a cab."

Jonathan stood on the curb and watched

as his fiancée flagged down a cab. He waved.

With both hands.

A week earlier he'd been in love with the woman he was waving to. Now, he didn't even like her.

His hand sought the silver picture frame. "Thanks," he murmured as he climbed into his car.

*"You're welcome."*

Jonathan whirled around so fast he got dizzy. "Margie?" When there was no response, he climbed into the car and turned on the ignition, then the lights. Before he slipped the car into gear, he withdrew Margie's picture from his pocket. "I guess it was wishful thinking on my part. I'm coming to see you now."

*"I'm waiting."*

He was overtired and hallucinating. Since Thanksgiving he hadn't been eating right and had barely slept two hours a night. The mind was a wonderful thing.

Fifty minutes later, Jonathan steered the

NO PLACE LIKE HOME

car off the Garden State Parkway at Exit 10. He turned onto Route 27, which would take him to Metuchen, New Jersey, where Margie was buried next to her parents.

A light snow was falling when he drove into the cemetery. He had the parking area to himself. Who in his right mind visited a cemetery at night? He hunkered into his cashmere coat and walked with his head down. He'd been there so many times, he knew he could find Margie's final resting place wearing a blindfold.

In the beginning, after Margie's death, they'd stayed at the apartment in New York for the Trips, even enrolling them in school just so they could make the hour-long trip to Metuchen every day. Back then, none of them could sleep unless they'd made the trip to their mother's final resting place earlier in the day.

It wasn't an overly large marker, but it was a meaningful one. Carved into the stone was a graceful angel, her wings spread just wide enough to encompass three small children. Their protector. Always their protector.

His cold fingers traced the outline of the angel and the children. A sense of peace washed over him. Marjorie Ann Cisco. And underneath, Wife and Mother. He dropped to his knees, his shoulders shaking. He talked then, saying all the things he hadn't said for years, things that needed to be said.

When he finally got to his feet, he was surprised to see that he was covered in snow. He felt numb with cold. His frozen fingers found the picture frame in his pocket. "I'm sorry. I took the wrong path, Margie. If it takes me the rest of my life, I'm going to get back on the right path. I just wanted to say I'll be back. I promise."

Tears rolled down his cheeks as he walked back to the car. He turned the heater on high. *"It's all right to make a mistake as long as you make it right in the end."* His fanciful imagination at work again? Maybe not . . .

# 7

~ • ~ • ~

Sam stopped the Rover at the top of the winding road that led down to the little valley where the cottage stood. For some reason, they always referred to the house as a cottage, probably because Cisco said it was originally supposed to be just a summer residence. Three rooms and a bath. Then, when their grandfather passed away, Cisco had had to sell the main house and move there with their father. Over the years, rooms and bathrooms had been added, although from this vantage point, those rooms weren't visible because they extended out the back.

The cozy cottage with the peaked roof was home.

They all climbed out of the car to stare down into the little valley. It was something they always did because it was so perfect, so beautiful. Now, with five inches of new snow covering everything, it was picture-perfect. Delirious with joy, Freddie romped and twirled and danced her way down the hill.

She was home.

"I swear to the Almighty, I am never leaving this place again," Cisco said reverently. "Do you hear me? Never!"

"We hear you, Cisco!" the Trips said in unison.

Excitement rang in Hannah's voice. "Everything's ready. We even found a handyman for you. His name is Ezra, and he lives over the rise. He brought a ton of firewood the other day. Sam invited him for Christmas Eve. He just moved here last year. He's a widower, Cisco, and he has a sweet tooth. He has a dog named Hugo. We told him he could bring him along."

"You are so shameless."

The Trips grinned.

"Power's on. For now. The generator is gassed up if it goes out. Phone's working. The fridge and freezer are full. Pump's primed. We're so golden, we glow!" Sam chortled.

"Did we tell you Ezra has a snowplow? Well, he does, and he should be here soon to plow the road. It might be nice to invite him for supper. I can't believe tomorrow is Christmas Eve."

Cisco dabbed at her eyes behind the dark glasses. "It looks like a Thomas Kinkade painting."

"No, Cisco. It looks like home." Sam wrapped his arms around his grandmother's shoulders. "We're going to Metuchen the day after Christmas, Cisco."

"I'll be right with you. Okay, let's go home."

A few minutes later, Sam held the front door for his grandmother. "Ohhh," was all she could say before the tears started to flow.

"You decorated the house! All our treasures," she said, looking around. "What a glorious fire! Oh, look," she said, sniffing into a wad of tissues. They all watched as Freddie dragged first her bed, then her blanket, then her toys to her spot by the fireplace. She looked up at her mistress before she made one more trip to the back of the house. When she returned, she was dragging a small quilt that she managed to nose up onto Cisco's chair, which was next to her bed.

"It's official, we're home!" Cisco said.

"Chili would be nice for dinner," Sara said.

"Apple pie would be really good," Sam said.

"A ton of garlic bread and some cider would be super," Hannah said.

"While I'm doing all that, what are you three going to be doing?"

They whooped as one. "We are going out to chop down the biggest, the best tree in the valley. We got the decorations out of the attic yesterday. We'll hang the wreath on the door when we get back," Sam said. "And don't touch those presents," he said, pointing to a pile of gaily wrapped gifts sitting in one corner.

"First, though, we're going to have some lunch. I want to sit in the kitchen and talk and just look at everything," Hannah said. "This is so much like old times, I feel like crying. Do you all remember how we sat here at the table and made that spindly Christmas tree out of popsicle sticks and painted it green? Then we made all those paper ornaments to hang on it. Then on Christmas Day, we piled into the car and drove five hours to New Jersey to put it on Mom's grave," Sara said.

"That's not something you ever forget," Hanny said, tears rolling down her cheeks. "Damn, why isn't Dad here?"

Cisco stared at her grandchildren. This was something they had to work out without her help. She started to bustle about the kitchen, making coffee and sandwiches, heating up canned soup. Outside a light snow was falling.

She walked over to the kitchen door, opened it, and looked down at the row of holly bushes. She felt like cheering when she saw the bright red berries through the snow. She continued listening to the Trips as she opened cans and jars.

"Hey, Sam, do you remember the time Cisco asked you to make a fire? You forgot to open the flue and the whole place filled up with smoke. Dad had to find us and drag us outside. We had to paint the whole place. We could have been overcome with smoke that day. I remember how he scooped me up under one arm, Hanny under the other arm, and you held on to his pant leg until we were outside. He seemed so big, so strong. so *fatherly*. He's not going to come, is he?" Sara mumbled.

"He might," Sam said. "Christmas is a time of miracles. Don't bet the rent on it, though." His voice was gruff and full of sadness.

Always in tune with her siblings, Sara turned to Cisco. "When everyone gets here, we're going to do all the stuff we do every year, right?"

"Of course we are. We're going to stuff the turkey, and, while it's roasting, we're going to make taffy. We're going to drink cider and eggnog, and sing carols while we decorate the tree. This year we're going to have so much help, it will all be done before we know it. It's going to be wonderful," Cisco said happily as she slipped Freddie a slice of cheese.

"Oh, no, Cisco, it has to take hours. *Hours.* That's half the fun. We're sticking to tradition here. Sara unwraps the ornaments, I hook them, you tell the story behind them, and Sam and . . . and Sam hangs them on the tree. We all get to open one present each. Lord, what a decision that is. Remember, Sam, the biggest isn't always the best," Hanny said. "Remember the time you couldn't wait to open that big box, the one the new washer came in, only to find a pair of wool ski socks. Boy, we had you going that year. You looked so dumbfounded. I will treasure that moment forever."

Cisco set lunch on the table. "It is like old times, isn't it?"

"It sure is. There is no place I'd rather be right now than here," Sam said. He bit into his sandwich. When no one was looking, he slipped Freddie part of it. Had he looked down at the floor, he would have seen that his sisters and his grandmother had done the same thing.

"I'll clean up," Cisco said, when they finished eating. "It's starting to snow again, so you'd better get out there and get that tree before we get six more inches of snow. Be sure to pick a nice one now. Freddie and I will stay here and wait for you. When you get back, I want you to cut some holly for the house."

When the door closed behind the Trips, Cisco walked over to her chair and sat down. Once more tears rolled down her wrinkled cheeks. "Thank You, God, thank You, God, thank You, God!" Freddie whimpered at her feet before she curled up on her bed. Her world was right side up, too.

Cisco sighed. She couldn't remember the

last time she'd been this happy. If only . . .
She sighed as she got up and stacked the
dishwasher.

It was an old sled, its runners polished to a
high gloss. The long rope handle was new. It
would take all of them to pull the tree back
to the cottage. They stopped twice, once to
make snow angels and once to pelt each
other with snowballs.

"So, when is the luscious Sonia due to arrive?" Sara needled.

"Listen, will you please not . . . give her
the business. She's shy, and she doesn't understand all the bullshit you two fling at me.
Will you just take it easy with her? I really
like her."

Sara and Hannah stared at their brother.
"Okay," they said in unison.

Sam eyed them suspiciously. "You're not
going to make me beg?"

"Nope."

"You aren't going to show her those bare-
assed baby pictures?"

"Nope."

"Why are you suddenly being so accommodating?" Sam asked suspiciously.

"So you don't turn around and do the same thing to Joel and Zack that you don't want us to do to Sonia," Hannah said.

"Aha!"

It started out as a playful punch to Sam's arm, then accelerated into a knockdown free-for-all. They battered each other, their faces furious, as they kicked, gouged, and shoved. It was a replay of their one and only battle after their mother died. Their father had tried to break that one up, but Cisco in her infinite wisdom had said they needed to get their grief and aggression out, and if it took a fight, so be it.

The name-calling now was more sophisticated and left no doubt as to its meaning.

Hannah's mittened hand went to her eye after Sara's fist landed a right hook. She toppled to the ground to roll over just as Sam took a wild, flying leap, his nose dripping blood. Hannah's foot went up and out, sending Sara reeling backward into the snow.

They screeched, they bellowed, they cursed as they refused to give up. When Sam landed in a snowdrift from Sara's wild swing, he thought his head was going to explode. "What the hell are we fighting about?" he managed to croak. "Damn, now I'm going to have a black eye. I can't see, and my head is ringing."

"Shut up!" Sara seethed. "I wasn't hitting you!"

"Take a look at my face and try telling me that again," Sam moaned. "Look at Hannah! Hey, are you okay?"

"Are you nuts! Do I look okay to you? I should kill you for hitting me like that. Don't give me any of that bull that you weren't hitting me."

Sara sat in a pile of snow hugging her knees, tears dripping down her cheeks. "Who the hell were we hitting?"

"Dad," Sam and Hannah said at the same time.

Sara snorted. They were right. "You two

look pretty ugly. You both have shiners. They'll go nice with your Christmas outfits."

"Wait till you see how you look," Hannah said, falling backward in the snow. She started to laugh then and couldn't stop. Sam rolled over on top of her, and, together, they rolled down the hill, their arms and legs going every which way. They were still laughing when they climbed back to the top of the hill.

"Your nose is three times its normal size, Sara." Sam guffawed. "Maybe one of those two dandy doctors coming for Christmas Eve knows another dandy doctor who can give you a nose job. You're gonna need it. Don't think for one minute your eyes aren't going to turn black-and-blue, because they are."

"Makeup . . ."

". . . Ain't gonna cut it, honey." Sam guffawed again.

"What the hell were we trying to do?" Hannah whispered as she packed snow around her eye.

"I guess we were . . . what difference does

it make?" Sara said, getting up. "C'mon, we have a tree to cut down."

"Do we really hate him that much?" Hard-Hearted Hannah whimpered.

"Nah. We just hate some of the shit he pulls. We can't hate our father. He's the only one we've got. I'm glad all those people are coming for Christmas Eve. Maybe we won't miss him as much." Sam pulled the string on the chain saw, but it didn't catch.

"We didn't pick out the tree yet. Why are you starting that thing up?"

"'Cause I'm going to chop off your legs if you don't shut up. Pick out a damn tree already. My eye's killing me. I wanna go home."

They trudged through the piney grove in snow up to their knees. "That's it! That's the one. It's perfect!" Sara said thirty minutes later.

"It's big all right," Hannah said, craning her neck to look up. "Do you remember the time . . ."

"Hanny, I don't want to play, 'do you remember.' I just want to get this tree cut so we can take it home. What are you waiting for, Sam?"

"Boy, are you ugly, Sara. Your nose is as big as Freddie's ball. You know, that rubber one she rolls around."

"Hannah, is it?" Sara wailed.

"It's big, Sara. How are my eye and cheek-bone?"

"You don't want to know."

"Timberrrr!" Sam yelled, shutting off the chain saw the moment the spruce tree fell to the ground. "Oh, it smells so . . . wonderful!"

"Yeah, it does. Wait till we get it set up in the house. The whole place will smell like it did when Mom and Dad put up the tree. Remember how sad Mom always got when we cut down a tree. She always made Dad plant *two* in the spring to replace it."

"I'm too tired to remember anything. Push, Hanny. Sam, come on, put some muscle behind it."

They were a quarter of a mile from the house when they stopped. "I can't move another step," Sam said. "One of you has to pull for a while, and I'll push. Hey, look, there's Ezra with his truck. Maybe he can tie the sled to the back and pull it."

The old man, seventy if he was a day, hopped out of the truck and looked at them. "Your grandmother sent me to find you."

"Well, you found us. Can you hook us up to the truck and get us home?" Hanny pleaded.

Arms like tree trunks reached down for the spruce. He had it up and in the back of the truck within minutes. The sled was next. "Hop in, young'uns."

"We still have to set the tree up in the living room," Sam gasped.

"Do you think we're dead and don't know it?" Sara asked as she poked her head out from between the branches.

"Who cares? We're all so ugly no one is ever going to look at us again. We must really look bad if that old guy didn't say a word."

Cisco and Freddie were standing in the

open doorway when Ezra pulled the truck to a full stop. "Last stop!" he called from the cab of the truck. The Trips piled out and staggered to the front door. Cisco looked at them and knew instantly what had happened. She didn't say a word, just stepped aside so they could enter the house.

She walked over to Ezra and placed a hand on his arm. "Just don't ask, okay? Now, if it isn't too much trouble, do you think you could lean the tree up on the front porch. We'll set it up tomorrow."

"Loretta, I'd be more than happy to set it up for you if you fetch the tree stand. It's my way of paying for my supper. You sure those young'uns are okay?"

"Ezra, they are more than okay."

A smile as big as the outdoors spread across her features when she walked into the living room. The Trips were curled into each other on Freddie's bed by the hearth, sound asleep. She brought her finger to her lips for Freddie's benefit. The golden dog sniffed, then walked away to join her new friend

Hugo, who was helping his master unload the tree from the back of the truck.

An hour later, Cisco looked at the magnificent tree and smiled. "You do good work, Ezra. I'm glad the Trips found you. I think it's just going to be you, me, and this lovely child Sonia for dinner. And, of course, our two four-legged friends."

It was six o'clock in the morning when Sam rolled over and bumped into his sister. He ached from head to toe. The fire was almost out. Why was he sleeping on the floor? Then he remembered. Hannah was the next to wake. She winced when she tried to stretch her arms and legs. Her gasp when she looked at her brother woke Sara.

They looked at one another, not sure if they should laugh or cry. As one, they bolted for the downstairs bathroom to stare at themselves. Hannah burst into tears. Sara turned away. Sam groaned as he limped out to the kitchen.

"Sonia!" he gasped to the small brunette

eating a stack of pancakes. "It's nice to see you. When . . . did you get here?"

"Yesterday afternoon. Sometime after your . . . accident with the Christmas tree. Your grandmother explained how you and your sisters risk your lives every year to cut down the family tree."

"Uh-huh," was all Sam could think of to say.

"My English is getting better, no?"

"Oh, yes, much better. You know Sara and Hannah," he said, pointing to his sisters.

"You are all very brave. I saw that tree."

"How bad is it, Cisco? Do we have anything that will help take down the swelling and discoloration?" Sara pleaded.

"I'm afraid not, dear."

Sara sat down at the table. "I really liked him. I wanted to impress him. I even bought this new dress. Veils, we can wear veils. We can say veils are the latest trend in fashion. They're guys, what do they know?"

"Shut up, Sara," Hannah said.

"I'm sure the young men will understand," Cisco said soothingly. "It's entirely possible they won't make it. Look outside. We got eight inches of new snow overnight. On top of the six inches we already had, that makes fourteen. I just heard on the radio that they are predicting another four to six inches this afternoon and into tomorrow. It's coming from Canada, I think. We might end up being snowbound. Run along now and get cleaned up. I'll have your pancakes ready when you get down here. By the way, Ezra was here earlier and brought gasoline for the snowmobiles. He's such a thoughtful man. I think we're going to become good friends. Freddie loves his dog Hugo."

The Trips tried to smile. It was what they wanted for their grandmother. They trooped off to return an hour later.

Cisco did her best not to smile as the Trips took their places at the table. Normally, they wolfed down her pancakes. Today, they barely touched them. "It's snowing harder," she said, pointing to the window. "I really don't think anyone will set out in this weather even if it is Christmas Eve."

"Maybe we could invite them for New Year's," Hannah suggested. "We'll probably look halfway decent by then. Please, please, let it keep snowing."

"I second that," Sara said.

Sam looked at Sonia, who was looking at him expectantly. "I'm so glad you could make it," he said, insincerity ringing in his voice.

"Sam, perhaps if you put a tea bag on your left eye, you might be able to open it a little," the elfin Sonia suggested. "A wet, warm tea bag. It is the tannin in the tea that has healing properties."

Cisco had a tea bag in her hand before Sonia could finish speaking. She held it under warm water, then handed it to Sam, who plopped it on his eye.

"Does that really help?" Sara queried.

"Not really, but it does take away some of the pain." Sonia smiled brightly for everyone's benefit.

"Sam, honey, I hate to ask you to do this, but we really need some firewood. I just used the last log off the back porch. We're going to be burning some serious wood today and into this evening. Bring as much as you can. You know how drafty this old house is."

"Sure, Cisco."

"I will help you," Sonia volunteered.

"I want to go to sleep and wake up January first," Hannah whined.

"Me, too. It's not going to happen, so let's get our asses in gear and start putting up the decorations. We have to hang the wreaths on the front and back doors. Cisco said she wants some holly brought in. Stop feeling sorry for yourself, because nothing is going to change."

It was noon when the last of the old decorations graced the cottage. "This was Mom's favorite piece," Sara said, setting a crystal angel on the coffee table. "Dad gave it to her the first year they were married. When and if we ever get married, which one of us is going to get it?"

"We'll take turns. You don't think Joel and Zack will make it, do you, Sara?"

Sara shrugged. "Depends on how much they want to see us. It is Christmas. No one wants to be alone on Christmas. Everybody wants to be with their family, except maybe our dad."

"They should have called by now if they aren't planning to make the trip. That tells me they're coming. It's too bad they had to go to that conference so they couldn't get here yesterday, when the roads were still okay."

Hannah's voice was so fretful, Sara started to cry. "I can see myself with Joel. I had this whole wonderful holiday scenario in mind. You know, mistletoe, Christmas spirit, cozy fireplace, everything smelling really good. I bought him a present. Nothing great, just a book on children, a cartoon kind of thing."

"I knitted a cap to go with the scarf I already gave Zack."

"Is it as lopsided as the scarf?"

"Yeah. At least they'll match. He'll never

wear them. I wrapped it pretty, though. I bought something for Dad, too. Did you?"

"Yeah. I found this old picture of him in Cisco's album. Someone took it when he was loading up her station wagon with candy. It's that brown sepia color. I had it blown up and put in a nice frame. What did you get him?"

"A picture of all of us. Mom's in it. Sam didn't get him anything."

"That's okay. He's not coming, so it won't matter."

"He might, Sara."

"No, Hanny, he isn't coming."

The phone rang. The sisters looked at one another. Each dared the other to pick it up. Finally, Hannah's arm snaked out. Her greeting was high and shrill. "What? I can barely hear you. Zack, is that you? Where are you? Oh! You're stuck in a snowbank. Can you give me better directions? Maybe you should turn around and go back. The weather is really bad and getting worse by the minute. You can't because you don't know where you are? I guess that makes sense. I know it's snowing. It always snows in the valley for Christmas. Bring brandy? I have no idea how long it will take us to find you. Oh, you're wearing my scarf and it's keeping your neck warm? You'll see us when you see us."

"Oh, God, they're coming, aren't they?" Sara wailed.

"They're lost. We have to go look for them. I know, I don't want to do that either, but we have to. They could die out there. He's wearing my scarf. He said it's keeping his neck warm. It's a good thing Ezra brought gasoline or they'd be in serious trouble. He must be intuitive. Ezra, I mean. Dress warm, Sara."

"Stop babbling, Hanny. You're making my headache worse."

"Who was that on the phone, girls?" Cisco asked?

"The guys. The doctors. They're lost. They're stuck in a snowbank. We have to go get them. We'll use the snowmobiles. Don't worry about us, Cisco. We know every inch of ground in this valley. We'll find them. You'll have to start the dressing for the turkey without us. Wait on the candy making, though. I'm not giving up that even for those doctors. Sam and Sonia can help you, and if you call Ezra, I'm sure he'll pitch in."

"Oh, dear. It's snowing harder, girls. Perhaps we should call the state troopers. What if something happens to you two? This is not a good idea. I just heard on the news that the roads are impassable," Cisco fretted.

Sam carried in the last load of firewood. "What's up?" he asked, looking from his grandmother to his sisters.

"Zack and Joel are stuck in the snow. We're going to take the snowmobiles to see if we can find them."

"You're nuts! You can't see an inch in front of your face. Cisco, don't let them go."

"If we don't go, they'll die out there. We have to try. Look, you know as well as I do that we know the terrain. If anyone can find them, we can. In the meantime, Cisco, just to be on the safe side, alert the troopers."

"Then I'm going with you. Just give me a minute to get my gear on. Don't forget the goggles; that snow stings when it hits your face. The temperature is dropping, too."

"Sam is so brave," Sonia said in awe. "First the ordeal with the Christmas tree and now this. You Americans are so . . . forceful. I love the way you take charge."

"That's us all right. Brave, forceful, and let's not forget, *stupid*," Hannah said as she pulled on her ski pants.

"The power might go out, Cisco. The generator is all primed. I showed Sonia how to start it up. You're all set. The stove will be fine because it's gas, so get that turkey going," Sam said.

The trio slogged their way through the snow to the barn. They had to shout to one another to be heard over the wind and biting snow that was taking their breath away. "That Ezra is something else. Look, he filled the tanks. Okay, let's go up the hill and run parallel with the road." He divvied up ten flares. His sisters jammed them into their pockets.

"Did they give you any indication how far away they were? How long were they driving? That conference was two hours from here."

"Zack said they left at ten o'clock. He called at noon. Two hours on the road but you can't go by that. The roads are hazardous, and they would have been driving slow. Who takes the lead?" Hannah asked.

"I will. Stay on my tail. Do you hear me? Don't veer off for any reason. These babies can really skim the snow, and we'll make good time. I suggest we stop every fifteen minutes to get our bearings. Keep your eyes on my headlight. If something goes wrong, send up a flare. If I'm in the lead, I won't know what's going on behind me," Sam said as he led his snowmobile out into the yard. He turned the key, the high-pitched whine of the engine grinding in his ears. He gritted his teeth at the symphony of sound behind him.

Cisco and Sonia watched until the little dots that were the Trips's headlights disappeared into the swirling snow.

Fern Michaels

On the second fifteen-minute break, the Trips had to scrape the ice from their goggles. "We're almost to the interstate. I'm thinking they ran into trouble when they hit the secondary road. Keep a sharp eye out. It's about eight more minutes to the exit where they would hit Ardmore Road. I'll send up a flare. You know how snow builds up on those curlicue curves. I bet five bucks they hit the shoulder and bounced into a drift. Stay close."

"I don't think I've ever been so cold in my life," Joel said as he blew on his hands. "Are we nuts or what?"

"Among other things. How come you don't have a shovel in your car? Most people around here keep shovels in their cars because it snows like this."

"Do you know why I don't have a shovel in my car, Zack? Because you borrowed it last night to dig out your car. You didn't give it back. That's why I don't have a shovel in my car."

"Is that a flare over there? Look, the snow

190

is orange. Yeah, yeah, it's a flare. Maybe it's the girls looking for us. Now, that's brilliant. Do you have a flare?"

"Do I look like I travel with flares? No, I do not," Joel said. "Turn the engine on and blow the horn. Lean on it!"

Zack did as instructed. The horn sounded feeble to his ears. He hoped the sound would carry on the wind to the person who set off the flare.

"Hey, do you hear that? Listen! Honk the horn again."

Zack obeyed his friend and colleague a second time as he pressed down on the horn. If he got any colder, he was going to snap in two.

When the snow turned orange again, they looked to their left to see three squat machines, their engines revving. "We aren't going to die after all," Joel said breathlessly. Once they were out of the car, the two doctors jumped up and down, their arms waving wildly. "Over here! Over here!" they shouted at the top of their lungs.

The Trips drove up to the stranded doctors, who looked like they might succumb to the cold any minute.

"Hop on," Hannah shouted. "Hold on tight."

"Oooh, I love it when you talk like that," Zack shouted in return as he squirmed and wiggled until he was comfortably seated on the snowmobile.

They waited until Joel was seated behind Sara.

"I'll take the lead. Same drill as before," Sam bellowed as loudly as he could.

They were back in the barn in less than forty minutes and in the house in less than ten. Hannah and Sara stayed behind to clean up the snowmobiles and lock up the barn. Their intent was to delay a face-to-face meeting—sans goggles, scarves, and wool caps—with the two doctors as long as possible.

Cisco immediately sent the two doctors upstairs and trailed behind them. She handed them thick towels. "Stand under that shower until you're warm. I'll send up some hot tea with brandy in it. Sam will give you some warm clothes. We're pretty informal around here on Christmas Eve. Aren't those triplets something? I called the troopers, but they were too busy with road accidents to look for you. I'd say you owe those three your lives."

"Those triplets are something, all right," both doctors agreed, their teeth chattering.

"There's one more small thing, gentleman. I have a favor to ask of you. It seems yesterday the Trips went out to chop down the . . ."

They listened intently. "We gotcha. Can we take our showers now?" Joel asked.

"Absolutely." Cisco dusted her hands dramatically as she made her way to the first floor. She had the situation in hand.

The Trips were standing by the old-fashioned stove, their faces pink from the wind and stinging snow. Sonia was rubbing aloe on their faces as she clucked her tongue in sympathy.

Sam was eating up the attention.

The back door blew open at the same moment Freddie raced through the kitchen.

"We're here!" Hattie shouted happily. "I didn't think we were going to make it, but we managed to get behind a snowplow the last fifty miles, and here we are!" John and Henry hugged the Trips while they waited their turn to be greeted by Cisco.

Cisco held out her arms to her old friends, crying openly as they hugged each other. "I was so afraid you weren't going to make it. I've been praying all afternoon for you to get here safe and sound. It must be thirty years since we had a snow like this in the valley. Everything is ready, but we're missing one guest. Alice was my nurse at the hospital. I hope she makes it. You three are just what these new eyes need. Will you listen to me. I'm just babbling here because I'm so happy to *see* you all. John, Henry, come here and give me a hug. You are truly a sight for these old eyes. It's just like old times, isn't it?"

"He's not here, is he?" Hattie whispered.

"No, Hattie, he isn't here. It's his loss is

how I have to think of it. We have extra guests this year, so they can take his place when we start to pull the taffy. This sweet child is Sonia, a friend of Sam's."

"Hello, Sonia. It's nice to meet you. Are you ready to help with the cooking? Let's do it.

"Who needs an apron?" Hattie shouted. When no one responded, she said, "Okay, no aprons." She turned to Cisco. "How do these young people cook today without smearing their clothes? I can't cook without an apron. Is everything ready?"

"No, no! We have to wait for the guys, and someone has to get out the eggnog and cider," Hannah said, her eyes on the doorway leading to the dining room.

Zack and Joel arrived right on cue. They smiled and didn't bat an eye when they took their places next to Hannah and Sara.

Sara looked up at Joel, her eyes miserable. "I look . . ."

"Sara Cisco, I don't care how you look right now. I really don't. You saved my life.

In the scheme of things, what's a few bumps and bruises? Come on, I want to learn how to make taffy. Tell me what to do."

Hannah, her eyes just as miserable, tried not to look at Zack. He cupped her chin in his hand. "I feel the same way Joel does, and I still want to marry you. You can wear a veil at the wedding." Hannah smiled through her tears.

The candy cauldron was cast iron and twenty-six inches high. It took three people to carry it to the stove once all the ingredients were added to the pot.

"When we were kids, we had to stand on a chair to stir the taffy," Sam said. "We all still have to stand on a stool so we can see down into the pot. We have to take turns stirring because the mixture gets thick and your arms get tired. We use this paddle. How old is it, Cisco?" he asked, pointing to a wooden paddle that was half as big as the paddle that belonged to his canoe.

"Decades old. It's the one I started out with. My son . . . my son made it for me because I had such a hard time stirring the candy once it started to cook up. See, he carved his initials in the handle."

Hattie stepped forward to cover the awkward moment. "I wish he was here," Sara whispered in Hattie's ear. Hattie nodded as she cleared the old table and rolled out sheets of waxed paper.

Hannah handed out cups of spiked eggnog just as the door opened to admit Ezra and Alice the nurse. Two small dogs raced into the kitchen behind Hugo. Freddie welcomed her guests and beelined into the living room to share her toys. "I found this lady stuck at the top of the hill. Sorry I'm late."

"You're just in time, Ezra. Would you like some eggnog?" Everyone greeted and hugged Alice.

"I really would, but the troopers called me to pick up a stranded motorist five miles up the road. Can you hold off till I get back? Shouldn't take me more than an hour, maybe not even that since I have the plow on my truck."

"All right, Ezra. Don't dawdle now. When the candy's done, it's done. If the motorist can't get to wherever he's going, bring him here."

The eggnog flowed, the kitchen rocked with laughter and good cheer as they all got in each other's way. The dogs enjoyed the Christmas spirit as they romped through the house. The house smelled wonderful with the scent of fresh balsam from the giant tree that still waited to be decorated, and the sweet, tangy scent of the candy bubbling on the stove.

The Trips looked at one another, their silent message to each other: I wish Dad was here.

Jonathan Cisco wondered if he'd die in the swirling snow. He'd been walking for what seemed like hours. He suspected he'd been walking in circles, but it was hard to tell. In his entire life, he'd never been so cold or so tired. His grip on the shopping bag was so fierce he knew his hands were frozen to the handles. He also knew he would die before he would part with the bag.

*Where the hell am I? How far from the cottage?* It could be miles, or he could be around the corner. He slipped and fell facedown in the snow. He wondered again if he was going to die. If he did, would they find his body? The spring thaw? If that happened, his children and his mother would never know how hard he'd tried to get home for Christmas. Maybe his mother would know since mothers were supposed to know everything. Margie always knew what he was thinking before he knew it himself.

He heard the sound before he actually saw the truck. It looked like a monster coming at him. He shouted, waved his hands, then fell facedown in the snow again. He heard a car door slam. *Maybe I'm already dead, and what I heard was the sound of the gates of heaven opening for me.* He struggled to his feet, then felt strong arms holding him upright.

"I gotcha, big fellow. Can you make it to my truck?"

"Yes, sir, I can make it. Where are we? I lost my bearings."

"Well, we're a piece down the road from my place. I live over the rise there. Name's Ezra. Down below is the Cisco cottage, maybe half a mile or so. I'd like to take you to wherever you're going, but people are waiting for me. Mrs. Cisco said I should bring you to her house. Where are you going, young fella?"

Jonathan started to laugh as he climbed into the truck. "I'm going to the same place you're going. I'm Jonathan Cisco. How did my mother know I was out here?"

"Oh, she didn't know," the man said, steering the truck around an icy bend. "The troopers called that someone was stuck and asked me to go fetch the motorist. Your mother said I should bring you, meaning the stranded motorist, to her house. It's Christmas, and the weather conditions aren't going to get any better. You feeling a little warmer now?"

"Yes, thank you. I'll make it up to you somehow, Ezra."

"No need to be saying that. When you do a good deed, it comes back tenfold. I'm going to park the truck. You go and skedaddle into the house and make your mama happy. Them triplets are going to be mighty happy to see you."

Jonathan stood outside in the cold and the snow, staring at the people milling around inside the kitchen. They were making candy. *I should be in there doing my share. Do I dare go in? Will they pitch me out?* He craned his neck to see if he recognized anyone. Hattie, John, Henry, his mother. A young guy with a god-awful-looking scarf around his neck, a bunch of young people. A pretty lady with soft brown hair wearing a bright red, reindeer sweater, two little dogs circling her feet. His eyes lingered on her a moment longer. Margie had had a sweater like that once. He shifted the shopping bag under his arm. His presents.

What would they do when he knocked on the door?

Well, there was only one way to find out.

He walked up the shoveled path to the kitchen door and then backed away three times before he could bring himself to knock. His heart was beating so fast he thought he was going to black out.

The door opened. Cisco smiled and held out her arms. "Merry Christmas, son."

He could barely get the words out as he hugged her until she cried for mercy. "Merry Christmas, Mom. I'm not too late, am I?"

"No. No, Jonathan, you're right on time. Let me introduce you to everyone. This is Alice. She's the nurse who took care of me when I had my cataracts done. Of course you know Hattie, John, and Henry. The man behind you is Ezra, my new neighbor."

The Trips stared at their father, their eyes filled with tears. They ran to him, almost knocking him over. "You came! You really made it! You're really here! We weren't going to put the star on the tree because you always do that." They hugged him, squeezed him, kissed him, their tears mingling with his.

"Candy's ready!" Henry shouted. "To your places! Jonathan, you're out of line!"

Jonathan shed his overcoat and hat, pushing up the sleeves of his sweater as he took his place in the line.

"Here it comes!" Henry said, as he, Sam, and John poured the candy onto the waxed paper. Hannah and Sara quickly worked the paddle from both ends, rolling the sticky candy back and forth. When they stepped back, Jonathan and Sam took the paddle and worked the candy across and down the table.

"Nice working with you again, Dad," Sam said in a choked voice.

His arms were so tired, Jonathan didn't think he could make his muscles work. But he'd die before he admitted it. "It's almost ready!" he shouted gleefully.

"Your turn," Sam said, handing the paddle to Zack and Joel.

"It's not budging." The doctors huffed and puffed.

"That means it's ready. Everyone butter your hands, get in a line, and start to pull.

Up, down, twist, then pull; up, down, twist, and pull," Cisco said.

"This is like the Keystone Cops," Hattie hissed in Cisco's ear.

"Yes, it is. Next year the newcomers will have a better feel for it. All things considered, we're doing rather well."

Forty minutes later, the candy was a solid three-foot-long braid of chewy taffy.

"When do we get a piece of this?" Zack asked.

The Trips stared at him in horror.

"What? What did I say?"

"We don't eat this. See that hole in the top! We put a string through it and hang it on a tree for the birds. All that butter and sugar will keep the birds warm when they nibble and lick at it."

"Oh. Who does that? I mean, who hangs it on the tree?"

"I usually do that," Jonathan said quietly. "If you'd like to do it this year, I'll grant you the privilege. I've had enough snow to last me a long time."

"We hang it on the old sycamore, so Cisco can see the birds from the kitchen window. Come on, put your jacket on and we can do it together," Hannah said.

"I'm glad you're tall enough to reach the branch," Hannah said, her teeth chattering with cold.

Zack tied the string of taffy securely on the branch. "When I was a kid, being tall was a bummer. I used to slump, and my mom would whack me good. She'd say, 'Zachary, stand tall!' It was a hard whack, too. This really is a wonderful thing, hanging this taffy for the birds. Everything is wonderful, your family, you. Especially you. My mother always told me when I met the right girl, I'd know it. Stupid me, I act to cover up my feelings. I liked you the minute I saw you looking up at me."

"I think I'm going to like your mother. I hope to get to meet her someday."

"Sooner than you think, Hannah. She's coming for New Year's. Your grandmother told Joel and me about your dad. Don't be too hard on him. From what your grandmother said, it seems he lost his way there for a bit. My dad kind of went off the deep end when my brother and I left home. He summed it up later by saying he felt like we didn't need him anymore. We did, just in a different way. Anyway, your father is here now, so be happy."

Hannah nodded and smiled. Zach took it as an open invitation to kiss her. It was the sweetest kiss of her life. She said so. Zack laughed as he wrapped his arm around her shoulder. "I think there's a waiting line for this taffy. Look!"

Hannah laughed out loud. "Merry Christmas, Zack." She waved her arms to invite the birds closer. "Merry Christmas to you guys, too." She reached for Zack's hand to lead him back to the house.

In the whole of her life, she'd never been so happy.

The kitchen was once more a muddle of bodies scurrying about. Each one had a job to do. Cisco issued her orders like a general, "Henry, set the dining room table. John, replenish the fires. Hattie, baste the turkey. Sara, wash the candy pot. Sam, you can dry and put everything away. Alice, you and Jonathan take the dogs out. Joel, you can peel the potatoes. Sonia, you cut up the salad. Ezra and I are going to sit here and have a cup of eggnog. When all your chores are finished, we're going to sing some carols, then we're going to decorate the tree."

"When can we open one of our presents?" Sam asked.

"When I say so and not one minute before," Cisco responded smartly.

Cisco felt Jonathan's hand on her shoulder. She reached up to cover it with her own. "Mom . . ."

"It's all right, son. You're here now. Our family is all together. That's the only thing that matters. Now, show Alice where the path is to take the dogs. Sam shoveled it earlier."

"This is a right nice family you have here, Loretta," Ezra observed. "I'm thinking I'd like to be a part of it. Gets lonely up on that hill with just Hugo for company. I think I might be spending a lot of time coming down here to get him since he seems so sweet on Freddie. We're of an age where it seems to me we shouldn't waste a whole lot of time."

Cisco chuckled, a rich sound of happiness. "I just might take you up on that offer. Did you bring me a present, Ezra?"

"I did. I made you a birdhouse that looks just like this house. Even painted it the same. When those grandchildren of yours hired me and told me what a special lady you were, I got right to work on it. I even wrapped it up. Did you get me a present?" he asked craftily.

"Of course. I knitted you a muffler and put your initials on the end. And I made you a cap to go with it."

Ezra beamed his pleasure.

Cisco smiled and smiled.

When the kitchen door closed for the last time, Cisco announced that it was time to adjourn to the living room. "Fetch the ladder, Sam. We're ready to decorate the tree."

They all gathered around the magnificent spruce tree. It was Hannah who started to sing "Silent Night," the others joining in. They were off-key, but no one cared. Sam swung into a lusty rendition of "Jingle Bells," and the old cottage rocked. Everyone knew the words.

The eggnog continued to flow, the fire blazed, and smiles were the order of the day.

Authority ringing in her voice, Sara said, "We do the ornaments assembly line–style after we string the lights. I unwrap them because they're precious, Hannah puts the hook on them, Cisco tells the story behind each one, then Dad and Sam hang them on the tree."

Jonathan said, "String out the lights and let's test them. I hope somebody brought extra bulbs in case some of them burned out.

Oh, here's a fresh box. We need the other ladder, Sam. One for the back of the tree and one for the front."

Sara moved away to open a battered cardboard box of ornaments. Joel held the box while she ripped at the masking tape to reveal a nest of tissue-wrapped ornaments. She looked up when Joel nudged her arm and pointed to the mistletoe hanging in the center of the doorway.

In a way it was an awkward kiss because they were both on their knees leaning over the box. In another way it was absolutely perfect and natural.

It was a wonderful kiss that spoke of promises yet to come. When Sara opened her eyes she saw Joel smiling at her. "I liked that," he said softly.

"I did, too. Can we do it again later? Sam hung mistletoe all over the house."

"Ah. A brother-in-law to be proud of. Oh, God, did I just say that?" Joel's face turned pink, to Sara's amusement.

"Uh-huh. Okay, everyone, stop gawking.

It's time to put on the ornaments. The last thing to go on the tree is the star. Dad climbs to the top of the ladder and hooks it on. It's not a big fancy ornament. It's papier-mâché, and our mother made it. It has a lot of nicks and flaws in it, and it's kind of tarnished, but it wouldn't be Christmas without that star. Would it, Dad?"

"No, it wouldn't," Jonathan said. "Well, let's get to it."

Cisco sat down next to Alice, who was watching the ornaments being put on the tree. "He's just like you said he was, Mrs. Cisco. My dogs like him, too."

"That's a lovely sweater you're wearing," Cisco said.

Alice smiled. "That's exactly what Jonathan said. He told me to call him Jon. This is all so wonderful. You have such a nice family, Mrs. Cisco. You must be very proud of them. Are you really going to move your company to Larkspur?"

"I am indeed. Even the corporate offices. That means Jonathan has to move back here.

I don't foresee a problem. Merry Christmas, Alice."

"The same to you, Mrs. Cisco."

"Everyone get ready!" Jonathan called out. "I'm going to turn on the lights. Get ready to oooh and aaah."

The tree was breathtakingly beautiful. The guests ooohed and aaahed on cue.

"Present time!" Sam shouted. "Please, Cisco, just one."

"All right. Just one each."

The young people were ten years old again as they dropped to their knees before a mountain of presents and shook, rattled, and poked at the gaily wrapped packages.

In the end, the Trips chose the three identically wrapped presents from their father as their choice. They cried and blubbered as they wrapped their arms around their father. Cisco smiled indulgently as she opened her birdhouse. Ezra was right, it was an exact replica of her cottage, right down to the three different chimneys. She turned to him and patted his hand. "We'll hang it tomorrow and fill it with suet. How do you like your muffler and cap?"

Everyone clapped when Ezra pulled on the cap and tied the muffler around his neck. He looked at Zack, and said, "Now, young fella, we both have one."

Zack undid the bright red bow on his package and pulled out the knitted cap that had a tail to it. He fingered the softness of the yarn, then tried to straighten it out. He pulled it on, the cap leaning drunkenly to the side. "I love it! It matches my scarf."

"I'll make you a sweater," Hannah said generously.

"I can't wait," Zack said.

The timer on the stove rang. Hattie took charge. "You young people continue with your gifts while the rest of us get dinner on the table."

Jonathan reached for Alice's hand. "We don't fall into that young people category. That means we have to help with dinner."

The Trips smiled at one another as they watched their father and Alice walk out to the kitchen. "It's perfect, just perfect." Sara sighed happily. "This is the best Christmas ever!"

"How long are you going to be here?" Joel asked.

"Till January 20, then we head back to school. Cisco is going full steam ahead with the move, so we'll be back for good in May."

"How would you like to take in a movie next week?"

"I'd like that. I really would."

"Do you believe in love at first sight, Sara?"

Sara looked over at the papier-mâché star in its nest of tissue paper. "My mother and father fell in love the minute they met each other. I guess my answer to your question is, yes."

Joel looked around. "Do you realize everyone here is paired off? Even the dogs. Do you think this is a coincidence, or do you think . . . ?"

"I think it's whatever we want it to be."

"Yeah, yeah, that's how I feel. Thanks for that baby book. That was very thoughtful of you. I love kids."

"I love kids, too. I love animals and I love my family and I love the whole world. Thanks for not saying anything about how I look. I really worried about what you would think. Hannah did, too."

"Your grandmother explained everything to us."

"Isn't she the greatest?"

"Yes, she is."

"Hey, whose turn is it to take the dogs out?" Sam bellowed.

"Yours!" Sara and Hannah bellowed in return.

Sonia was on her feet in the blink of an eye, searching for her coat and Sam's.

"Don't look at me, Sam, I'm not loaning my scarf and hat to you!" Zack fell over laughing at the look on Sam's face. "If we get married in the wintertime, I can wear it to the wedding," he said to Hannah.

In the kitchen, busy as they were, they all

stopped for a moment to listen to the wild laughter in the living room. Cisco looked at her son and smiled.

"Merry Christmas, Mom. Merry Christmas, everyone!"

"Merry Christmas!" the young people shouted from the living room.

# Epilogue

≈ · ≈ · ≈

*Thirty-one Months Later*

*L*oretta Cisco thought her heart was going to burst right out of her chest. Just two short years ago, she'd stood here with her family in exactly this same spot and watched the ground-breaking ceremonies for the new Cisco Candies factory. Now, she was here with her family, her dear friends, her employees and some of the town's dignitaries waiting for her son Jonathan to cut the yellow ribbon that would signify Cisco Candies was, after a short hiatus, once more making candy. But this time they were making it in Larkspur, Pennsylvania.

The best part, she decided, was the old warehouse she'd purchased, then renovated for the company's headquarters. On a good day, if the weather conditions permitted, and her knees held out, she could take Freddie for a walk and visit both places.

Her cup indeed runneth over.

She reached for Ezra's hand. As Hattie put it, they were keeping company these days. She smiled because it sounded so wicked.

"It looks to me, Loretta, like your family is the happiest family in the valley these days. I've never seen your son so relaxed and contented. I'm thinking that's because of Alice and those two pups of hers. Do you suppose they'll marry?" Ezra asked.

Cisco looked up at her beloved mountains, all the way to the top of the tree line. "I think Jonathan is going to take it slow and easy this time around. The Trips gave their seal of approval, so that's a plus. Alice is in no hurry either. They have a deep, comfortable relationship, the kind you and I have, Ezra." Ezra nodded approvingly.

The Trips rushed over the moment the ribbon cutting ceremonies were over.

"The first shift starts at seven tomorrow morning," Sam said. "I think John and Henry are going to sleep in the factory tonight. They're arguing over which one is going to turn the switch on. I think it's going to be Hattie because she looks like she has a secret. They do like to devil one another. It's beautiful, Cisco. Everything is new and modern. All your employees are happy to be here, not to mention the hundred and fifty new employees from town. Best move you ever made, Cisco." Sam wrapped his arms around his grandmother.

"I think so, too. We're open and ready for the Christmas season. It seems strange to say that in the middle of summer. Are the orders coming in?" Her voice sounded more anxious than she intended.

"Hot and heavy," Hannah said. "New orders are coming in every day. "We aren't going to miss a beat."

"Sending out all those brochures we had made up, all the renderings of the new building, was a stroke of genius on Hannah's part," Sara said. "She did it all. People like warm and cozy. People like comfort and stability. They love small towns. Customers like knowing we sponsor Little League and give out scholarships. It makes them feel like they're part of our company. It's a win/win situation, Cisco," Sara said.

"Well, I think Ezra and I can head back to the house now. I can see I'm leaving my company in good hands. I just wish you three would get married already," Cisco sniffed.

"New Year's Day is the big day. That's just a few months away. You know what? I can't wait myself." Sara gurgled with happiness as her eyes sought out those of her intended. Joel waved.

"Sonia's whole family is coming from the Ukraine for the wedding. They don't speak *any* English. None," Cisco said.

"Now, that's where you're wrong, Cisco. Sam is teaching them via the Internet. He said by the time they get here they will be fluent."

"Want a ride home, Cisco?" Hannah asked, her hand in Zack's.

"It's magnificent, Mrs. Cisco. I want to thank you again for moving your business here. It would have been hard courting a girl who works in New York."

Cisco laughed. "I kept that in mind the whole time."

"Mom, are you leaving already? Aren't you going to stay for refreshments?" Jonathan asked.

"No, son. You do the honors. You're the boss now. Ezra and I have some things to do back at the house. I promised to bake him a blackberry pie. Freddie and Hugo are waiting for us."

Her family watched her walk away, her hand in Ezra's. Tears rolled down the Trips's faces. Jonathan bit down on his lip so he wouldn't cry the way his children were.

"Why do I feel like this is the end of something?" Hannah cried.

"Look, she's just walking away from us," Sara sobbed.

"She doesn't need us anymore," Sam said, his voice so choked up, the words ran together.

Jonathan finally found his voice. "She's always been the wind beneath our wings."

Alice did something then that stopped all of them in their tracks. Hands on hips, she eyed them one at a time. "Shame on all of you. How selfish can you be? These are not Loretta's golden years. These are her platinum years. Didn't you hear what she said? She said she promised to bake a pie for Ezra. Right now that's the most important thing in the world to her. The dogs are waiting for them. She was there every step of the way for all of you. She gave you this," Alice said waving her arms about. "It's her turn now. It would be nice if you could be happy for her."

Bug-eyed, the Trips stared at Alice. "You

sounded just like Mom when you said that," the Trips said in unison.

"That's exactly what Margie would have said," Jonathan said quietly.

Cisco turned around and waved. "See you on Sunday for dinner," she called.

"Okay," they shouted as one. "We'll be there."

And they would be there, because there is nothing more important in the world than family.

# A Conversation with Fern Michaels

**Q: After forty-four best-selling novels, what inspired you to write *No Place Like Home*, your first holiday novel?**

For starters, I'm the oldest kid I know when it comes to Christmas. I start planning in July. Christmas is a time when people are kind, mellow and a sense of family is on everyone's mind. I'm as big on family as I am on Christmas. I also had a grandmother whom I loved dearly. Like Loretta Cisco, the grandmother in *No Place Like Home*, she lived in a little cottage, too. I guess I was trying to relive that time in my life in some way because it was so wonderful.

**Q: Are the Michaels family holiday festivities anything like the Cisco family's festivities?**

Absolutely. We do it all. We start around four

o'clock on Christmas Eve and go to whenever.

**Q: *Do you have a favorite holiday tradition you perform every year?***

Yes. I have five children, three grandchildren and five dogs. I wrap up thirteen silly presents and hide them outside. I pray there's no snow so tracks don't show. It's kind of like an Easter Egg Hunt at Christmas. For some reason, the kids consider those presents the most important ones. The dogs get in the act, too, because I wrap up beef hides and they can smell them.

**Q: The taffy-pulling scene in the novel seems wonderfully authentic. Did you rely on firsthand experience when you wrote it?**

Yes, but that's what we used to do for Halloween when the kids were little.

**Q: Is there a special holiday recipe you make every year?**

My daughters always come over early and we start cooking. We make everyone's favorite food. Being Polish, my family's favorite is pierogi.

**Q: What is your favorite Christmas carol? How about your favorite holiday song?**

My favorite carol is "Silent Night." My favorite song is "I'll Be Home For Christmas," sung by Bing Crosby. And "Jingle Bells." We really sing that one with a lot of gusto.

**Q: Why do you frequently feature dogs as significant characters in your novels?**

As a child I wasn't allowed to have a dog. As soon as I was on my own, I got one. When I got married, I got more. They're smart, they're loyal, and they love unconditionally. I'm an Animal Rights Activist and do what I can for all kinds of animals. Dogs, though, are my dearest love.

**Q: Going back to the subject of the holidays, let's get down to brass tacks. Do you and your family open your presents on Christmas Day or Christmas Eve?**

That is a biggie. When the kids were little, we did it on Christmas morning. When Santa got stuck in the chimney for the last time, we switched up to Christmas Eve. That was about thirty years ago. We pile all the presents in the middle of living room early on Christmas Eve morning. The kids deliver all theirs and the mountain grows. After a big dinner, we start opening them, but the stockings and all their treasures have to wait until Christmas morning. It usually takes us four hours to open them all. It's a ritual that everyone has to hold the present up, say who it's from so everyone can oooh and aaah and then they go home and leave me with the mess. They pick up their presents Christmas Day when they come for brunch. That's when it all gets cleaned up. We get two bites at the apple that way by looking at all the presents again.

**Q: *No Place Like Home* is set primarily in Pennsylvania. Your next novel, *Late Bloomer*, is also set there. Is that a favorite spot?**

You bet. I was born and raised in Pennsylvania. Right at the base of the Allegheny Mountains.

**Q: Your next novel is about . . .**

A young woman who is searching for the answer to a tragic childhood accident that left her near death. In her search for the answers, she rekindles old childhood friendships. The only problem is . . . the childhood friends are all grown up now and those childhood friends have a secret. A secret they're afraid to share with her. With the help of a fearless canine, a well-meaning geriatric trio (her grandmother being the ringleader), and the local police chief, our Late Bloomer plunges head on into ferreting out her friends' deadly secret.

**Q: What was the biggest challenge in writing *Late Bloomer*?**

Sometimes a character takes on a life of his or her own. I couldn't decide which of the good guys should end up with my girl. One of them wasn't supposed to be as good as the other but in the writing, he turned out really nice. I didn't have the heart to turn him into something else. I always fall in love with the main guys.

**Q: Finally, is there one special wish you would like to have come true this Christmas?**

Yes. It's the same wish every year. It's what all my kids wish for, too. We wish and hope that no more animals have to be put to sleep for lack of funding, and that they're all safe and sound because they are God's creatures, too. If I was allowed a frivolous wish, I'd wish for naturally curly hair.

Please turn the page for a preview of
Fern Michaels's
Cisco family novella

# FAMILY BLESSINGS

Available from Pocket Books

# Chapter One

"IT'S HARD TO BELIEVE HALLOWEEN HAS COME and gone already." Loretta Cisco, founder and recently retired CEO of Cisco Candies who was known as Cisco to her family, opened the screen door to let the dogs out. Freddie, a golden retriever, barked to let his partner, Hugo, know it was time to get a move on. It was the same thing as saying the breakfast bacon will still be there when we get back. Hugo, a black Lab, bolted through the door.

Ezra Danford, a tall, robust man, and Cisco's live-in companion, as well as partner, turned from the stove where he was making blueberry pancakes, Cisco's favorite breakfast. "I know what you mean, Loretta." He insisted on calling her by her given name, saying the pet name Cisco was just for her son and her grandchildren, the triplets, to use. "In a few weeks we'll be out there raking the last of the leaves and bringing in firewood. Then before you know it, the holidays will be here."

Cisco tugged at the apron she was wearing. "Time moves too fast when you're old, and we're old, Ezra. I dearly love the holidays, as you well know, but in another way they're sad because it means another year is coming to a close. You and I, my dear, also have an anniversary coming up. If the Trips," she said, referring to her triplet grandchildren, "hadn't brought you here that special Christmas almost three years ago, I might never have gotten to know you. For that, I will be eternally grateful."

Ezra expertly flipped a pancake, then turned the strips of bacon to the other side. "We should get married, Loretta." He winked at her, hoping she would get flustered and say yes.

Cisco adjusted the glasses perched on the end of her nose before she gave her colorful apron another hitch. "No, Ezra, we shouldn't get married. You had a wife, and I had a husband. When we depart this world, you're going with your wife, and I'm going with my husband. That's the way it has to be. Otherwise, your children and grandchildren will have a problem, as will mine. They won't know where to put us.

"We've talked about this a hundred times, Ezra. Why are you bringing it up again today? The relationship we have right now is working just fine for both of us. You know what happens when you tamper with something that doesn't need tampering with."

Cisco took her place at the table, the dogs' plates in her hands. Her gaze was drawn to the kitchen window. "Is it my imagination, Ezra, or does it look yellow outside?"

A puzzled look on his face, the man, who was as big as a bear, walked to the old screen door and opened it. It did look yellow outside. His eyes narrowed slightly. "Loretta, turn on the television or radio and let's hear the weather report. There might be a fire somewhere. I don't hear the birds either. It's much too quiet," he said, peering into the distance. "I know it's autumn, but it's strange. The winter birds love to nest in your old sycamore and sing to us every morning when we have breakfast. Some bad weather might be on the way." He called both dogs to come indoors.

"Are they saying anything on the TV?" Ezra walked out onto the back porch and looked around. The air was yellow as far as he could see. He stepped back in and looked at Cisco questioningly as the dogs whined at her feet.

Cisco poured syrup on her pancakes. "They haven't said a thing. We'll keep it on while we eat in case a bulletin comes in. We can't have bad weather today. The family is coming, and we're picnicking under the sycamore. A nice, long, lazy Sunday to enjoy having everyone here with us. It will probably be our last outdoor get-together before the cold weather sets in. There simply cannot be any bad weather today. I won't allow it," she said lightly.

Ezra ate quickly, something he never did. He loved food and always took his time when eating, enjoying every mouthful. When he finished, he picked up the dogs' plates and his own and stacked them in the dishwasher before he walked back to the door to stare at the yellow world outside the house.

He moved then, quicker than lightning. "Hurry, Loretta. I want you and the dogs to go down to the root cellar. I can't be certain about this, but the only time in my life that I saw a world of yellow was when I lived in Arkansas, and a tornado whipped through. Hurry now."

Cisco needed no second urging. She dumped her dishes in the dishwasher and herded the dogs down the cellar steps. "What are you going to do, Ezra?"

"Lock up, crack some of the windows. I'll be down in a minute. Take care of the dogs. Go to the southwest corner of the root cellar. Maybe I'm wrong, Loretta. It's better to be safe than sorry."

Cisco was at the bottom of the steps when she heard the sound. She knew instantly what it was. "Never mind the doors, Ezra, get down here. Now!"

Ezra was at the bottom of the steps the minute she finished speaking. The dogs whined and whimpered as Cisco led them down three more steps to the root cellar, where she kept her winter vegetables. The door was stout, with iron bars crisscrossing it from top to bottom.

The sound overhead increased in volume until it sounded like a hundred jet airplanes breaking the sound barrier. Ezra and Cisco clung together, their old bodies trembling as they tried to comfort one another and the dogs at the same time.

And then it was deathly quiet. The dogs yipped once, then were quiet.

Ezra struggled with the iron bars holding the door in place. When he finally got the door open, he was looking at the cellar staircase and nothing else. He could see the sky, the backyard, and the old sycamore. He tested the steps to make sure they were sturdy before he allowed Cisco and the dogs to climb them. He went first, ascending the steps carefully.

He looked around in stunned amazement. It was all gone, every last wall and window. What looked like half of the roof was on top of the barn, which itself was leaning drunkenly to the side. There was no sign of Cisco's car or his pickup truck.

Ezra's voice sounded choked. "This house was in the direct path, Loretta. It's all gone. Look up the hill; my house is still standing."

"It can't be gone, Ezra, it just can't," Cisco insisted as she looked around. She started to cry. Freddie hugged her leg, not understanding what was going on. Hugo pawed Ezra's leg for the big man to comfort him. "My whole life was here in this little house, Ezra.

All the Trips' belongings were here as well as my son's from the day they were born. How can I ever replace them? Oh, Ezra, this is the worst thing that's ever happened to me. It's worse than when my son stuck me in that assisted-living facility. At least I could close my eyes and picture this beloved little house of mine. How can it all be gone, Ezra? *How?*"

All Ezra could do was put his arm around her shoulder, and murmur, "I don't know, Loretta. I just don't know. Careful, watch your step now. Let's take a walk around. Maybe we can salvage something."

"I'm too old to start over, Ezra. Do you see my kitchen table anywhere? I started Cisco Candies in my kitchen on that old table. I kept the Trips' bassinet in the kitchen because it was the warmest room in the house during the winter. I diapered Jonathan there, too. Oh, God, how did this happen?" She looked around wildly as she staggered from one place to another, hoping to find something that belonged to her.

Ezra's voice was gentle, soothing, when he said, "You can rebuild the house and barn, Loretta. A good contractor can have it built for you by Christmas if the weather holds. I wouldn't be surprised if the whole town turns out to rebuild for you because you moved Cisco Candies here from New York City and provide employment for so many of the people in town. We can stay at my house while the building is going on. I know that's not what you want to hear, but it's the only consolation I can give you right now."

Cisco gave no indication she could hear what he was saying. Instead, her gaze raked the yard, hoping to see something from the house. She hated the way she was feeling, hated the tears rolling down her wrinkled cheeks. Her voice was a whisper when she said, "Where do I go to get my memories back? I need to *touch* my things. I need to *see* them." She picked up the hem of her apron and wiped at her eyes. "Why, Ezra, why?"

Ezra wrapped his arms around her, his eyes full of sadness. "No one can take away your memories, Loretta. Your mementos, yes, but not the memories. It was an act of God, and we're both wise and old enough not to question Him. Now, pull up your socks, old girl, and let's walk around. I'm sure we'll find something."

"One thing, Ezra. All I want is one thing. Something to hold in my hand. Please, help me. Please. I can't believe this. My whole life was in that house, and now it's gone. It's like it was never here. Like *I* was never here. It was here one minute, then in another minute it was gone."

Ezra linked his arm with hers. He squeezed her hand to give her comfort. Together, they started off, their steps wobbly and unsure, the dogs trotting along beside them.

"We're in the valley, Ezra, why did it hit here and not the top of the hill where your house is? Why are the gardens and trees intact? I don't understand any of this. Look at the pumpkins! Even the leaves haven't been damaged. The holly trees are just as beautiful; so is the sycamore. Just my little house. Dammit, Ezra, this isn't fair!"

There was no answer, and Ezra didn't try to find one. All he could do was help Loretta search for her belongings.

"Freddie can't sleep without her blanket," Cisco said brokenly as she picked her way through debris. "I need my pillow. You need your slippers. You just got them broken in so they don't hurt your bunions."

"We'll buy new ones, Loretta. One can get used to anything. We're all alive. That's all that matters. Tomorrow we'll call a contractor I know and a salvage company. We're going to rebuild your house just the way it was. Maybe even better. Life will go on, Loretta, because that is the order of things. Now, I'm going to ask you one more time, and I'm never going to ask you again, so keep that in mind when you give me your answer. Will you marry me?"

Cisco stared up at the big man whom she loved so dearly. She was aware, for the first time, how vulnerable she was. She would never, ever, take anything for granted again. If it hadn't been for Ezra and his keen eye, they'd all be dead. "Yes, I will marry you on Christmas Day," she responded smartly.

"Attagirl! Whoa, what have we here?" Ezra said as he heard the dogs barking furiously. "Follow the sound, Loretta. I don't know this for certain, but I think the dogs found something."

They ran as fast as their seventy-year-old bodies would permit. Cisco's disappointment was so keen, Ezra felt it. "It's my yellow teakettle. Look, the whistle is still on it. It wasn't exactly what I had in mind to hold in my hand, but it will do. I think it's as old as I am. Good girl, Freddie," Cisco said, reaching for the battered teakettle. "Where's Hugo?"

As if on cue, the black Lab trampled through a hedge of mountain laurel, dragging a string of Christmas lights. He dropped them at Cisco's feet and barked happily.

Cisco gathered up the string of lights with her yellow teakettle and held them close against her chest as though they were a lifeline. "I wonder if the lights work. We have to go to your house right now, Ezra, and plug them in. If they work, I think I can handle the rest of . . . *of this.*"

"Let's walk a little more, Loretta. We might find something else." The expression on Cisco's face made Ezra do an about-face. "On second thought, let's walk up to my house and turn on the television. We might as well find out the bad news now. I'm sure there were other houses in the path of the tornado. I want to see if those lights work, too. Christmas Day is going to be extraspecial this year, eh?"

Cisco squeezed Ezra's hand. "Yes, and I'm going

to wear my old wedding dress. Hannah made me a white shawl last year for Christmas, and I'll wear it, too. Do you have your old wedding suit?" She started to cry again when she realized her old wedding dress and the white shawl were gone, along with everything else.

"I do! It might be a tad snug, but I'm game if you are."

A tired smile worked its way around Cisco's lips. "My dress would have been too snug anyway. Hannah and Sara wore it and had it taken in when they each got married. Their mother wore it, too. That old wedding gown had a lot of mileage on it. Do you think that's the order of things, too, Ezra? You know, the way it's supposed to be?"

Ezra didn't know if it was or wasn't. He opted to take the high road, and said, "I suppose." Cisco seemed satisfied with his answer as they trudged up the winding road to Ezra's house. The dogs scampered ahead, barking joyfully, certain this was a new adventure.

Inside Ezra's sparkling kitchen, Cisco looked around. "I don't like this kitchen, Ezra. It's right off the assembly line. It's so . . . so . . . *modern*. There's no character here, no memories. It's just a house. Why is that, Ezra?"

"Because it's only four years old. It's new, Loretta, built to my specifications. New is new. You and I can build a few memories here until it's time to move into your *new* house. It might be a good thing for both of us. Nothing is forever, as we just found out. What are you doing, Loretta?"

"I'm scrubbing the teakettle so I can make us a cup of tea. We have to have tea, Ezra. To . . . to . . . seal . . . oh, I don't know. I just feel like making us tea. Did you plug in the lights?"

"Yes! Turn around!"

"Oohhh, Ezra, they work. They actually work!

How beautiful they look. Just looking at them makes me feel better. They have to be at least fifty years old, maybe more. Wrap them in tissue and put them somewhere safe. The Trips will want to see them. They are going to be so devastated when they get here."

"They're young, Loretta. I'm not saying they'll take it in stride, but they'll adjust better than you and I. Let's face it, we're set in our ways," Ezra said as he turned on the small television on the kitchen counter.

Cisco looked at him, a sour expression on her face. "What you mean is *I'm* set in my ways. Tell me something. Why do you need all these fancy appliances? Sub-Zero this, Sub-Zero that. What's wrong with Sears Roebuck appliances?"

Ezra threw his hands in the air. "I don't know, Loretta. The contractor installed them. I wasn't even here when the house was being built. You'll get used to them in time, and if you don't want to cook, then I'll cook. Oh, listen, they're talking about the tornado."

Cisco turned on the gas and set the yellow teakettle on the burner. They both stared at the television, their faces filled with horror. The news wasn't good. Seven houses in the path of the tornado were leveled. Four people were dead. Three people were missing. Seventeen cars simply disappeared off the face of the earth. Volunteers were asked to report to the school gymnasium to help aid the homeless victims. The Red Cross would be setting up a command center at City Hall.

"We can't even go into town to help since our cars are gone," Cisco said sadly. "As soon as the Trips get here, we'll go and do what we can. We . . . I don't have anything to donate, but I certainly have enough money to help out. Hannah is so good at doing things like that. We can put her in charge. Sara, too. Sam can scout around for living accommodations for the homeless, and I'll pay the rents. Zack and Joel can offer medical services since both of them are doctors.

Jonathan . . . well, Jonathan can work on the transportation end of things. We're part of this community, and we have to do everything we can.

"Did you think Hanny looked *twitchy* last week when she stopped by? And Sam was almost surly. I wonder if it's my imagination. I always knew what was going on with my grandchildren, but since they all got married I'm . . . what is it the young people say these days? Out of the loop."

Ezra scratched his head. Sometimes Loretta moved and did things at the speed of light, and he had to struggle to catch up. "As I recall, Hanny did seem a little jittery. Is it possible she's pregnant? Sam now, that's something else. I think he's struggling with something, and, whatever it is, he's holding it close to his chest. At least for now."

"No, Hanny is not pregnant. When you're pregnant, you're so beautiful you just glow. Your eyes sparkle with happiness. Hanny doesn't look like that. I don't know, Ezra, maybe she's having trouble adjusting to being married. After all, she's only been married ten months." Cisco couldn't help but smile as she remembered the triple wedding that took place last New Year's day. Hannah had wed Zack Kelly, the ophthalmologist who had removed Cisco's cataracts at Larkspur Community Hospital; Sara had wed Joel Wineberg, a pediatrician affiliated with the hospital; and Sam had married Sonia, the Ukranian exchange student he'd fallen for at Penn State. What a memorable day it had been. So much happiness. Now, she turned her gaze back on Ezra, and said, "As you know, my granddaughter Hannah is tart-tongued. The children called her Hard-Hearted Hannah from the time she was little. She takes no prisoners. Hanny is a 'what you see is what you get' kind of person. She wasn't like that during our visit. She was quiet and spent a lot of time staring out the window. I think she's worried about something.

Sam . . . I just don't know." She shook her head in bewilderment.

Ezra was grateful Loretta was talking about something other than the loss of her beloved little house in the valley. Having raised the triplets after their mother's death, she was more mother than grandmother to them and worried constantly even though they were twenty-five years old. Some things, he knew, would never change.

He wished his own children, who lived in California, were closer to him. He told himself they had their own lives just the way his grandchildren had their own lives. They called on Father's Day and Christmas, but that was it. He'd been stunned when Loretta and her little family had welcomed him with open arms. He could still remember her words as if it were yesterday. "I'd be more than happy to share my family with you, Ezra. We have more than enough love to go around. One more will fit very nicely into our lives. And, we adore your dog!" He'd actually blushed, then felt like beating his chest in some primal way to show how much he'd come to love them all.

He needed to say something reassuring to Loretta now before she got carried away. She was right, though, Hanny hadn't been herself the last time she visited. "I think Hannah is like most young people, Loretta. She's busy and tries to fit everything into a twenty-four-hour period when she really needs thirty-six hours." He didn't want to think about Sam because Sam worried him, and he didn't know why.

"I have an idea. The family isn't going to be here for a few hours. They may not even know what happened yet. What do you say to my getting out the old tractor mower and we take a spin into town? It'll be slow going, probably around three miles an hour or so. We should get there around noon if we leave now. You might want to pack a lunch." Ezra guffawed. If he was hoping for a laugh or a rich chuckle from Cisco, he was disappointed. She was a million miles away in her memories.

"All right, Ezra. We might even meet up with the Trips while we're there. Just let me get changed. What *does* one wear for a ride on a tractor into town?"

Ezra eyeballed her to see if she was trying to be humorous or not. He decided she wasn't. "I suppose whatever one can find. You do have clothes upstairs, Loretta."

"I know, Ezra, I know. I'm sorry I'm not acting . . ." Her voice trailed off to nothing.

"Loretta," Erza said patiently, "I know how you all loved that little house. As hard as it is for you to believe or understand, you have to make the effort to come to terms with the loss. Everything happens for a reason. Most times a person never finds out the reason until much later, then they go, 'ah, now I understand.' Tomorrow the sun is going to come up, and we'll decide what to do. Your family will be arriving soon, and you'll want to discuss matters with them. For now, we'll just muddle through."

Cisco reached up to touch Ezra's cheek. "What would I do without you, Ezra? I don't care about the sun coming up tomorrow. Well, I do, but I just want you to know that you are the sunshine of my life. After everyone leaves this evening, I'm going to bake you a wonderful blackberry pie, and you and I are going to eat the whole thing."

Ezra smiled. "I thought the family was staying overnight."

"Well, we'll just have to shoo them out. You don't have enough room in this house for everyone. I'm going to bake you that pie, and that's final."

"With ice cream and vanilla-flavored coffee?" Ezra asked hopefully.

"Absolutely," Cisco said. "I'll be ready in a few minutes. Get the mower out. We have to leave the dogs here of course."

Ezra knew she was just going through the motions and saying words she thought he wanted to hear. "I'll get the mower." If Cisco heard him, she gave no sign.

Two hours later Ezra steered the John Deere tractor mower down Main Street. No one paid them the least bit of attention.

Nestled in the foothills of the Allegheny Mountains, Larkspur was a pretty little town with a town square where all public functions were held. The Fourth of July picnic was always a rousing success, with banners and American flags everywhere and a hundred percent turnout of the citizenry. The parade down Main Street was full of homemade floats, the school band, the football team, and baton twirlers.

Hot dogs, hamburgers, corn on the cob, and root beer slushes were the food and drink of the day. At night, from seven till nine, there was a square dance in the pavilion for the older folks. From nine to eleven, the pavilion was turned over to the younger set and a local band named Fred Fish and the Merry Minnows, which the youngsters rocked and rolled to until they were dizzy. It was the highlight of the year.

Then again, the older folks said that Christmas was the highlight of the year, with the live Santa, who sat in his sleigh for twenty-one days, handing out candy canes until the moment that the carolers took over on Christmas Eve, when, once again, the whole town turned out, this time to join the carolers before going to midnight services at the churches that held them.

It was a sleepy, comfortable little town, where everyone knew everyone else. A town where people cared about their neighbors and offered to help the minute things went awry, which wasn't often.

Today, the town was a beehive of activity, with television trucks, satellite dishes, and news media there to cover the deadly tornado.

"The last time I saw this many people in town was the Fourth of July," Cisco said, as Ezra helped her down from the mower. "I think we should find the mayor and go from there. What do you think, Ezra? I don't see the children anywhere. We should have left a note on your door. Why didn't we do that, Ezra?"

"We just forgot, Loretta. Come along."

"I'm coming, Ezra, hold your horses," Cisco shot back with a smidgin of her old spirit.

The blue BMW wound its way down the road, then accelerated up the rise. When Sara Cisco Wineberg reached the crest, she sucked in her breath and let out a scream that could be heard from one end of the valley to the other. "Look, Hanny! Oh, my Godddd!"

Hanny opened the door and started to run, Sara on her heels. "The house is gone!" she screamed shrilly. "Where are Cisco and Freddie? Sara, say something. Tell me they're all right. Please, tell me they're all right," she continued to scream shrilly.

Sara started to cry. "How can I tell you something like that?" She started calling out to her grandmother, but there was no response. "I heard about the tornado on the news, but I never thought . . . I just didn't think . . . oh, God, not Cisco. Someone should have called us. Come on, Hanny, we have to look for them. It's gone," she babbled. "It's all gone. Even the fireplace is gone." She called out again, this time more shrilly. Hanny joined in.

"Why didn't they call us to say they were okay?" Hanny bleated. She picked up a stick and whacked at a sapling. "I don't see any of our stuff. What happened to the washing machine? The refrigerator, our beds, the furniture? Did they just fly through the air? What? Dammit, I need to know, Sara."

Sara sat down on a tree stump and stared up at her sister. She was already hoarse from all the shouting. "I don't know the answer, Hanny. I don't know much of anything these days. My husband should be here; so should your husband. And where the hell is our brother Sam? It would be nice to see Dad, too. They must have heard the news like we heard it, so why aren't they here?"

Hannah sat down on the ground and hugged her knees. Like her sister, she was hoarse from shouting. "Let's go up to Ezra's house. Maybe they're up there It's still standing, I can see the roof from here. They aren't dead, Sara. I'd feel something if they were, and so would you. But, to answer your other question, I don't know why my husband isn't here. He had to work today, even though it's Sunday. That's all he does, work. I hardly ever see him. Sam said he was leaving early to come out here. Maybe he's with Cisco and Ezra." She stood up and reached for Sara's hands to pull her to her feet.

Sara sprinted off, her mouth going a mile a minute. "Please let them be alive and well. Please, please, please."

"Where's Joel?" Hannah asked at the halfway mark up the hill.

"The same place your husband is, the hospital. I never see him, like you never see Zack. This marriage business isn't what it's cracked up to be. I cook dinner and eat it by myself. I go to bed by myself. When I wake up, Joel is gone. He leaves me notes. I thought it would get better, but it isn't. I'm seriously thinking about asking for a divorce. I can't live like this anymore. How do you do it, Hanny? Oh, God, is that Freddie barking? It is! They're here! They're here, Hanny!"

They both ran then, across the yard and up the long driveway, as though they had wings on their feet. They skidded to a stop when they saw a dark green Range Rover crawling up the hill behind them.

"Sam!" the girls said in unison.

"Yep, it's me. I've been down in the valley searching. I found this," he said, holding out a yellow ribbon with a bell on it."

"That was my first hair ribbon. Mom put a bell on it so she could find me," Sara said, bursting into tears. "She said I always wandered off."

"Freddie's here, so that has to mean Cisco and Ezra are here, too. They wouldn't have left the dogs alone. They're safe, I know it," Sara said, breathing hard. "Can't you hear Freddie barking?"

Sam climbed out of the truck. He was dressed in jeans and a white T-shirt. His curly hair was cropped short and smashed down with a Pittsburgh Pirates baseball cap. "That sound is music to my ears. When I pulled up to the rise earlier, I almost died when I didn't see the house. I think I went a little nuts there for a minute."

"So did we," Sara said. "Where's Sonia?"

"She's packing to go back home. That's another way of saying she's leaving me. Now, do you want to talk *that* to death, or do you want to find Cisco and Freddie?" Sam asked, his tone of voice frigid.

Hanny stopped in her tracks. It seemed to her in that one instant that her whole life was unraveling. The house was gone, Cisco and Freddie were missing, Sara was talking about getting a divorce, and now Sam was saying Sonia was leaving him. On top of that, she had her own miserable problem with Zack to deal with.

"Divorce is such a terrible . . . ending. I thought you were happy," she muttered.

"I was. Obviously, Sonia wasn't. Is the door locked?"

"Get real, Sam. No one in Larkspur locks their doors. Open it!"

The dogs leaped and pawed at them, barking joyously as Sara ran through the house searching for her grandmother. She was back in the kitchen within minutes. "They're not here, but Cisco's clothes are. Maybe they had enough time to get to the root cellar, and when it was over they came up here. Cisco must be devastated. Hell, I'm devastated. Dad's coming, isn't he?"

Sam was on the floor, Freddie in his lap. He stroked the silky dog, his eyes moist. "He said he was."

Hanny turned on the television to the local station. The trio sat and watched, their eyes wide with the devastation they were seeing. "Nothing like this has ever happened around here."

Sam's voice was so bitter-sounding, his sisters cringed. "There's a first time for everything, I guess."

Hanny thought about her brother's words. A first time for everything. It was so true. She bit down on her bottom lip. The urge to cry was so strong, she bit down harder and tasted her own blood. "You're right, Sam. There's a first time for everything."

She jumped up, jamming her hands into the pockets of her khaki slacks.

"You look like you lost some weight, Hanny," Sara said.

"Well, I didn't. It's your imagination. I eat like a horse," Hannah lied. She couldn't remember the last time she'd eaten a solid meal.

Sara blinked, her expression confused. "Hey, I just made a comment, okay? You don't have to bite my head off."

"Sorry, Sara. I'm just worried," Hannah said.

"Now that that's out of the way, let's pile into my Range Rover and go to town to see if Cisco is there with Ezra. I'm thinking they'd both go there first thing to see if they could help. C'mon, guys, let's go," he said to the anxious dogs. "It's time to find Cisco."

## #3417 THE SICILIAN'S STOLEN SON
### by Lynne Graham
Jemima Barber promised to look after her troubled late twin
sister's son. So when the boy's father turns up to reclaim the
child, Jemima pretends to be her seductress of a sister...until
Luciano Vitale discovers she's a virgin!

## #3418 THE BILLIONAIRE'S DEFIANT ACQUISITION
### by Sharon Kendrick
For Conall Devlin to complete his property portfolio, he's willing
to accept an unusual term of the contract...taming his client's
wayward daughter! And Conall's plan is to offer Amber Carter her
first job—being at his beck and call day and *night*...

## #3419 SEDUCED INTO HER BOSS'S SERVICE
### by Cathy Williams
When widower Stefano Gunn met Sunny Porter, he was sure
of two things—she was the perfect person to take care of his
daughter *and* the most sinfully seductive woman he's seen! And
in this game of seduction he *will* win...

## #3420 ENGAGED TO HER RAVENSDALE ENEMY
*The Ravensdale Scandals*
### by Melanie Milburne
Jasmine Connolly decides to make her ex-fiancé jealous by
enlisting the help of her enemy, Jake Ravensdale! But behind their
fake relationship tensions build as the line between love and hate
increasingly blurs, teetering on the brink of explosion!

HPCNM0316RA